methuen | drama
LONDON • NEW YORK • OXFORD • NEW DELHI • SYDNEY

METHUEN DRAMA
Bloomsbury Publishing Plc, 50 Bedford Square, London, WC1B 3DP, UK
Bloomsbury Publishing Inc, 1385 Broadway, New York, NY 10018, USA
Bloomsbury Publishing Ireland, 29 Earlsfort Terrace, Dublin 2,
D02 AY28, Ireland

BLOOMSBURY, METHUEN DRAMA and the Methuen
Drama logo are trademarks of Bloomsbury Publishing Plc

First published in Great Britain 2025

Cover design by Bob King Creative

Cover photography by Manuel Harlan

Bloomsbury Publishing Plc does not have any control over, or responsibility
for, any third-party websites referred to or in this book. All internet addresses
given in this book were correct at the time of going to press. The author and
publisher regret any inconvenience caused if addresses have changed or sites
have ceased to exist, but can accept no responsibility for any such changes.

No rights in incidental music or songs contained in the work are hereby
granted and performance rights for any performance/presentation
whatsoever must be obtained from the respective copyright owners.

All rights whatsoever in this play are strictly reserved and application
for performance, etc. should be made before rehearsals by professionals
and by amateurs to United Agents, 12–26 Lexington St., London, W1F OLE.
No performance may be given unless a licence has been obtained.

A catalogue record for this book is available from the British Library.

A catalog record for this book is available from the Library of Congress.

ISBN: PB: 978-1-3505-6397-1
ePDF: 978-1-3505-6398-8
eBook: 978-1-3505-6399-5

Series: Modern Plays

Typeset by Mark Heslington Ltd, Scarborough, North Yorkshire

For product safety related questions contact
productsafety@bloomsbury.com.

To find out more about our authors and books visit
www.bloomsbury.com and sign up for our newsletters.

The Score by Oliver Cotton originally premiered at Theatre Royal Bath in 2023 before transferring to London's Theatre Royal Haymarket where it opened on 20 February 2025.

Bach	Brian Cox
Anna	Nicole Ansari-Cox
Carl	Jamie Wilkes
Frederick	Stephen Hagan
Emilia	Juliet Garricks
Voltaire	Peter De Jersey
Quantz	Christopher Staines
Benda	Toby Webster
Graun	Matthew Romain
Helstein/understudy Carl & Frederick	James Gladdon
Soldier/understudy Helstein	Will Kerr
Soldier/understudy Quantz, Benda & Graun	Jordan Kilshaw
Maidservant/understudy Anna & Emilia	Rebecca Thornhill
Von Meckelsdorf/understudy Bach & Voltaire	Geoffrey Towers

Director	Trevor Nunn
Set and Costume Design	Robert Jones
Lighting Design	Johanna Town
Composer and Sound Design	Sophie Cotton
Associate Director	Cordelia Monsey
Casting Director	Ginny Schiller CDG

The Score

Characters

Johann Sebastian Bach, *sixty-two*
Anna Magdalena Bach, *forty-five*
Carl Philipp Emanuel Bach, *thirty-four*
Frederick II, *King of Prussia, thirty-five*
Emelia, *an old servant, sixty-seven*
Johann Joachim Quantz, *a court composer, fifty*
Franz Benda, *a court composer, thirty-eight*
Carl Heinrich Graun, *a court composer, forty-three*
Voltaire, *fifty-three*

Act One

Scene One

Leipzig. Saxony. May 1747. Thomasschule, Bach's second-floor apartment. Early morning. 5.00 a.m.

A wide room. Large windows look out onto a small park below and the river Pleisse. Heavy rain beats on the window.

Three travelling bags lie nearby.

Johann Sebastian Bach, *sixty-two, stands at a table, sorting through a sheaf of manuscript pages. An earthenware jug of coffee stands nearby with two cups and some bread rolls.*

Johann *wears spectacles, but he still squints to focus. He organises some of the pages into a neat pile and then pours himself a cup of coffee.*

Drunken shouts are heard from the park outside. **Johann** *moves to the window taking his coffee with him. He peers down An angry scream is followed by the clash of swords.* **Johann** *winces and moves away.*

Returning to the table he puts the pile of manuscript pages into a folder. He then picks up one of the travel bags, places it on the table and stuffs the folder inside.

Johann's *wife* **Anna Magdalena** *enters from a door that leads to a staircase. She wears a nightgown but has added a robe for warmth. She looks exhausted.* **Johann** *pockets his specs.*

Johann   How is she?

Anna   Still very hot. I gave her a wash.

He makes for the staircase.

Anna   Don't go up. She's sleeping. Berthe's with her.

Johann   When's Doctor Klein coming back?

Anna   Probably this morning. But he said he's not concerned.

Johann   He wasn't up all night with her –

More shouts outside and a cheer.

Anna   What's that?

Johann   They're duelling.

Anna   At five in the morning?

Johann   With sabres. There's a crowd of them watching. They're all drunk.

Anna *crosses to the window. A scream of pain from outside and then yelling from a small crowd of men. Running feet. Someone shouts an order.*

Anna *recoils in disgust. Sits at the table. Puts her head in her hands.* **Johann** *looks briefly out of the window again.*

Anna   I don't want to live like this.

Johann *pours her some coffee. Passes her the cup.*

Anna   What time is your carriage?

Johann   Six. But I don't think I should go. The roads will be a quagmire.

Anna   Did Fiedler come for your trunk?

Johann   He can always bring it back.

Anna   Johann, you were supposed to go two days ago –

Johann   Well, another day won't –

Another shout from outside. He goes to the window. Looks out.

I'll go tomorrow.

Anna *stares at him. Her voice has a trace of panic.*

Anna   I think you should go today.

Johann   I just said – I'll go tomorrow.

Anna   Johann – you're driving me insane. Yesterday it was the row with Kraus, the day before that some nonsense about the consistory –

Johann   I don't want to go. Not with Regina like this –

Anna   Dr Klein said –

Johann   I don't trust Klein –

Anna   Johann, it would be a mistake not to go. I know the Prussians.

A shout from below. He gestures to the window.

Johann   You think I don't!

Anna   This is a *royal* invitation! And it's the fourth one! You've made excuse after excuse.

Johann   They weren't excuses. I was genuinely unable to go –

Anna   But now you can. You accepted. Why do that if –?

Johann   I accepted three months ago! Things were very different.

Anna   I don't understand why you've waited until an hour before your coach leaves to –

Johann   *Because I don't know my own mind!*

Anna   Please, don't shout!

Johann   I didn't sleep. I lay there all night – praying for guidance. These troops have turned our city into a filthy, drunken cesspit – and I'm travelling a hundred miles to kiss their king's arse –

Anna   You don't have to kiss anything – other than your son. Carl's expecting you. His children are expecting you –

Johann   Don't be ridiculous. His children are barely two years old –

Anna   The King of *Prussia* is waiting for you.

Johann   He'll get over it.

He looks out at the rain.

Anna   Yes. It's raining! You've seen rain before – and you've travelled in worse than this –

Johann   But if this keeps up it'll take three days – the axle could break, wheels fly off . . .

Anna   It's *two* days. My guess is you'll be in Luckenwalde by this evening.

Johann *points into the air.*

Johann   Oh, look! A pig!

Anna *bangs the table.*

Anna   Johann. Listen to me. To refuse him again will be seen as an insult. For sure. Understand that. He wants you there because he sees you as the greatest composer in Europe –

Johann's *temper snaps.*

Johann   Rubbish! He's a tiddle-arse flautist who collects serious musicians to flaunt before his tiddle-arse court – that's when he's not decimating whole nations, or randomly occupying their cities!

Anna   Ssssh! Please! Johann! Someone will hear you!

Johann   Nobody calls a composer 'the Great', do they? But massacre thousands, torch their farms, desecrate their churches, bayonet their children, make every tree a gallows – and the world calls you 'Great'. Frederick the Great!

Anna   Yes, and he's easily affronted. So don't affront him. Please.

Johann   And, if I go then what do I tell the council here?

Anna   Why should the council know where you've been?

Johann   They'll find out.

He smashes his hand down on the table in frustration. **Anna** *jumps in shock. She buries her face in her hands and starts to weep.* **Johann** *goes to her.*

Johann   Anna –

Anna   I'm sorry – I'm exhausted. But I mean it. These are not ordinary times – and I'm frightened . . .

Johann *puts his arms around her.*

Anna   Please, Johann, go! Go to Potsdam. It's only four days – and you never know, this tiddle-arse flautist may give you a commission! You'll make the right noises – you'll keep your temper – you'll spend time with Carl, you'll see his new babies, and you'll be back before you know it. Just in time for some serious eye surgery with that nice Dr Taylor.

Johann   Oh God!

Anna *nods sympathetically.*

Anna   And the blind shall see. Something else to vacillate about.

The sound of running feet below in the park. A shout.

Anna *gets up. She goes to a drawer and takes out some food wrapped in a muslin cloth.*

Anna   For the trip.

Johann *takes the food parcel and goes to the stairway door. Stands listening.* **Anna** *watches him.*

Anna   Please. Don't wake her up.

Johann *nods. He puts the food into one of the travelling bags, goes to* **Anna**, *takes her hands and they kneel together on the floor, their heads bowed.*

Anna   O God, our heavenly Father, whose glory fills the whole creation, and whose presence we find wherever we go: Preserve those who travel; surround my husband with your loving care; protect him from every danger; and bring him in safety to his journey's end; through Jesus Christ our Lord. Amen.

Johann *reaches out and gently pulls her face close to his. Still kneeling, he kisses her on the mouth for a long time.*

Then he helps her up, picks up the bags –

Anna   Do you have your glasses?

He pats his coat pocket. **Anna** *holds up three fingers.*

Anna   How many fingers am I holding up?

Johann   Eleven.

She grins. He blows her a kiss – and leaves. A child's cry is heard from upstairs. **Anna** *makes for the staircase. From outside – the rain increases, more swordplay, more shouting and the sound of running feet.*

Scene Two

Two days later. Prussia. The palace of King Frederick II. Potsdam. Evening. May 1747.

An elegantly furnished room with three large casement windows. The furniture includes a wardrobe, a tall chest of drawers, a round table, some comfortable chairs and a bureau. Wall hangings surround a portrait of King Friedrich Wilhelm I.

A door leads to a bedchamber.

Somewhere far away a bugle blows and a voice shouts orders; the distant echo of marching feet is punctuated by more screaming, more drill.

There are four men in the room.

Johann Quantz, **Heinrich Graun**, **Franz Benda**, *and* **Carl Philipp Emmauel Bach**. *All four are composers in the employ of King Frederick II. There is an end-of-day atmosphere of informality and relaxation.*

Quantz *and* **Benda** *sit at a table finishing some food and wine.*

Graun *tinkers at the clavier, worrying away at the same phrase of music – ten notes played in different combinations – over and over again.*

Carl *stands staring anxiously out of the window.*

Quantz *is in the middle of telling a joke. He's a good storyteller and he snacks while he talks.* **Benda** *listens entranced.*

Quantz   So, he's teetering on the edge of the cliff – staring down at the rocks . . . a thousand feet below . . . and he's getting dizzy . . .

His attention is caught by a phrase that **Graun** *is playing.*

Quantz   Play that again . . .

Graun *plays the sequence of notes again.* **Benda** *sighs with irritation.* **Graun** *fiddles with the sequence some more –*

Benda   Oh, come on! He can do that in a minute. The man's staring down a thousand feet drop . . .

Quantz   Oh yes – sorry . . ., when, all at once – whoosh – he's blown straight over the edge . . .

Benda   Oh my God!

Quantz   Yes . . . aaaaahhh – down he plunges, he's an instant from death – but – there's a root sticking out from the cliff – and he grabs it and – Whaahaaaah! It nearly rips his arm off . . . and somehow, don't ask me how, he manages to hold on . . . And now he's – dangling from the root, his feet scraping the chalk, the rain splashing his face – above him, the sheer face of the cliff – and all around, the screaming wind. There's nothing he can do. Nothing. He screams up the cliff face – 'Helloooo! Is anybody there?'

There's no reply. He tries again – 'Help! Help! Hello-ooo! Is anyone up there?' And then – the most extraordinary thing . . . the rain stops. Just like that! So does the wind. And – there's silence. Absolute silence. And then – out of nowhere – there's a voice. A deep and compassionate voice. It seems to come from everywhere at once. 'My son. Do not be afraid. Let go of the root. Allow yourself to fall. I will catch you – and I will raise you – up, up, up to safety. Trust me. Do it now. Let go.' . . . The man can't believe what he's hearing! What to do? Total indecision, total crisis, Total paralysis! Then, in a blinding flash, it comes to him –

Benda   Yes?

Quantz   He lifts his head and bellows up the cliff: 'Is there anybody else up there?'

Benda *and* **Graun** *gasp – then they laugh and applaud.*

Benda   Brilliant!

Graun   That's very good . . .

Benda   It is. And His Majesty told you that?

Quantz   Yes. He told the whole orchestra!

Carl   Weren't they shocked?

Quantz   They're used to it. Anyway, what could they do?

Carl   Exactly. You tell it very well, but . . . it might be an idea to avoid that kind of joke in front of my father. That's if he ever gets here.

Graun   Would he be offended?

Carl   Depressed, more like.

Graun   Depressed?

Carl   I haven't seen him for nearly two years but . . . I think so, yes.

Quantz   Why?

Carl   Well, the joke's all about doubt.

Benda   Is it?

Carl   Well, isn't it? A desperate man hears the voice of God and doubts what he's hearing –

Quantz   Carl. It's a joke!

Carl   I know! About doubt. I don't give a damn but –

Graun   But surely your father's faith transcends such trivia?

Carl   He wouldn't see it as trivia. Doubt depresses him. It makes him anxious.

Quantz   Oh.

Carl   Doubt in faith, that is.

A beat.

Quantz   So. Not funny.

Carl   I doubt it.

He realises what he's said and he shrugs with a wry smile. **Quantz** *grins.* **Graun** *is trying another note sequence.*

Graun   Listen to this.

Quantz *starts back to the clavier.* **Carl** *makes for the door.*

Quantz   You're not going out there again?

Graun *resumes playing.*

Carl   Well, I can't just stand around in here . . .

Benda *gets up.*

Benda   Carl. Listen. It must be pretty obvious by now that –

Quantz   Maybe a wheel came off? Maybe they're stuck in a stream? Maybe a passenger was taken ill and –

Benda   That happened on my coach to Dresden. I spent two hours sitting next to a corpse . . .

Carl   Thanks.

Quantz   There's no point speculating – but standing at the gate won't get him here any faster. Have a drink.

Carl   I don't want a drink. I'm not standing at the gate and I'm not staring down the street.

Quantz   I didn't mean it literally. I just think you should –

Benda   Carl, it's understandable. You're worried. I would be too – in fact, I am. I am worried. All we're saying is –

But **Carl** *has moved back to the window.* **Benda** *looks to* **Quantz** *in some confusion. What did I say?* **Quantz** *gestures for him to leave* **Carl** *alone.*

Quantz *turns his attention back to* **Graun***.*

Quantz   Where are we? Play it from the start.

Graun *starts back on the ten-note sequence. However, he doesn't get very far before the door opens and an old servant woman,* **Emelia***, enters. She is carrying several bags.*

Emelia *is followed by* **Johann Sebastian Bach***.* **Carl** *stands rooted to the spot.* **Johann** *flings his arms wide.*

Johann   Carl!

Carl   Oh my God!

Father and son share a heartfelt embrace.

Carl   We've been waiting since this morning. What happened?

Johann *waves a dismissive hand. He staggers to a chair and sits heavily.* **Quantz** *pours him some wine.*

Johann   Don't ask. We were stopped five times. Five times! Twice yesterday, three times today. Customs!

Carl   Ah. Yes, well things are tense . . .

Johann   Get any tenser nothing will move at all! The last time was just outside Treuenbrietzen. Nasty little man, strutting around in the rain. Mouth like a dog's arse. 'All out. Bags down, empty your pockets. Papers, papers, let's see your papers.' I completely lost my temper. I said, 'You Prussians can't fall into a ditch without showing your bloody papers. And when you get out you have to show them again.'

Quantz *laughs and hands him the wine.* **Emelia** *collects up the used crockery and puts it on a tray.*

Carl   Oh God . . .

Johann   He didn't like that. I said, 'And that's another thing – you people never laugh, do you? Not unless someone's hurt themselves.'

Carl   Listen, Father, I can see this must have been –

Johann   I thought he was going to hit me. So I pulled out the letter, showed him the King's seal. Opened it up. God! You should have seen him. Turned into a slavering dog. Crawling, whining, wetting himself. 'Oh, Herr Bach, forgive me. I'd have let you through but we have our orders.' I said, 'What's your name?' And he said, 'Helmut something' – so I said, 'Listen, Helmut. This goes straight to His Majesty. You understand? I shall make a full report. He'll see your stupid name and that will be that. Do you understand? That will be that!'

Carl   Will you report him?

Johann   Can't be bothered.

Carl   Anyway, I doubt it was customs.

Johann   Who then?

Johann   Probably secret service. They're convinced the King will be assassinated.

Johann   Well, he's certainly going the right way about it. Who's going to assassinate him? The Austrian Queen?

Carl   Something like that.

Johann   Well, I'm with her. After what he did to Silesia.

Carl   Shhh! For God's sake! He has agents everywhere.

Johann   Are you one?

Laughter. **Emelia** *steps forward, tray in hand.*

Emelia   Would Herr Bach care for some supper?

Johann   Thank you. Yes.

Emelia *bows and retires, taking with her the tray full of dirty dishes.*

Carl   Father, allow me to introduce my esteemed colleagues.

Johann *rises.*

Quantz   Please, Herr Bach! Sit. Sit.

Johann   No, no. I wouldn't think of it Herr Quantz.

Quantz *holds out a hand.* **Johann** *takes his hand and the two men bow to each other.*

Quantz   We have been waiting eagerly all day for your arrival. I'm afraid we were about to –

Johann *looks to the other two. Gives a little bow.*

Johann   Herr Benda? – and Herr Graun?

The two men flush with pride at being recognised.

Benda   Herr Bach – this is a great honour. I have admired your music for so many years –

Johann   And I yours, Herr Benda. Only yesterday, I was humming a movement from your violin concerto – the one in A major. Came into my head.

Benda   My –? I'm sorry – but where did you hear it?

Johann   Sadly, I don't think I ever did. But I was fortunate enough to get a glimpse of the published score a few years ago.

He sits down at the harpsichord and plays a few bars from the concerto's first movement. **Benda** *is staggered.*

Benda   Note perfect!

He throws his arms wide in amazement.

Quantz   And this from viewing a score? Once? Several years ago?

Johann *shrugs.*

Johann   I loved what I read – and I have a reasonable memory. That's all.

Carl   No doubt my father will play all your published works as well, Quantz, but now I think –

Quantz   Of course! Of course! Forgive us, Herr Bach – you must be completely exhausted.

Still at the harpsichord, **Johann** *starts to play again.* **Quantz** *steps back in amazement.*

Quantz   But that's my –

Johann   – flute concerto?

Quantz   It is!

Johann   In G minor. I heard such a wonderful performance of it.

Quantz   When?

Johann   In Mannheim. I don't remember the name of the flautist but –

Quantz   Mannheim? But . . . I was the flautist!

Johann   What an extraordinary thing! Well, you see how memorably you played!

Quantz   And you were in the audience?

Johann   Not exactly. I was waiting outside the hall. I had arrived too late – once again! I listened at the door. I remember the piece very well. Beautiful!

He plays a few bars more of what must be the slow movement. **Quantz** *stares at him in mystification.*

Carl   Gentlemen –

Graun   Yes, yes – we must allow you to eat and rest –

Johann   And later, perhaps we can discuss your opera, *Caesar and* . . .

Graun   *Cleopatra*? You know it?

Johann   I saw it, in Berlin. Must be five years ago, but it could have been yesterday . . . I remember so much of it. Your music was superb. Unforgettable.

Emelia *enters bearing a tray of food and wine. She lays the food and cutlery on a small table.*

Quantz   Ah! Supper! We'll take our leave, Herr Bach.

Benda   Yes. Rest well and –

The three composers bow.

Quantz   Goodnight, Herr Bach.

Benda   Goodnight.

Graun   Goodnight.

Johann *bows – and they leave.* **Emelia** *has finished laying out the food. She gives a little bow and leaves.* **Carl** *gestures to his father to sit and eat.* **Johann** *ignores him.*

Johann   So. What's my programme?

Carl   Programme?

Johann   When do I meet the King?

Carl *shrugs.*

Johann   You organised my visit.

Carl   I didn't organise your visit. I wrote a few letters!

But I have no idea when he plans to receive you. Sorry. I'm not his secretary. Could be in five minutes. Could be five days.

Johann   I'm only here for *four* days.

Far away, a bugle blows. **Johann** *stops. Listens. More bugle calls.*

Johann   Does that go on all the time?

Carl   What?

Johann   That!

A drum beats in the distance. More marching, more screaming, more drilling.

Carl   Day and night.

Johann *goes to the window.*

Johann   Doesn't it drive you insane?

Carl   After five years I hardly notice it.

Johann   It seems to be coming from everywhere at once!

Carl   There are barracks for miles around. And there's a military academy at Babelsberg –

Johann   But it's so late.

Carl   I know. It's past their bedtime.

Johann   I've never heard soldiers at this hour.

Carl   Welcome to Prussia.

He starts to put food on **Johann**'*s plate.*

Carl   Come on. Eat.

Johann *sits. Starts to eat hungrily.*

Carl   How is it?

Johann *talks with his mouth full.*

Johann   I shouldn't be here. I should have gone straight to Berlin, spent some time with my granddaughter and then straight home to Leipzig.

Carl   You will see her. In three days.

Johann   I know but I should never have come here.

Carl   So why did you?

Johann   Not brave enough to refuse the King of Prussia.

Carl *laughs.*

Carl   God knows you've tried . . .

Johann   But vain enough to want his approval – and greedy enough to want his fee.

Carl   Is there one?

Johann   You never know. Depends on the size of his commission. What's worse is – half the Leipzig council suspect I'm here. It's barely two months since the dregs of this despot's army arrived –

Carl   Shh! For God's sake!

In some paranoia, he moves stealthily to the door. He yanks it open. There is nobody outside. He closes the door. Talks in a whisper.

Carl   Please. I'm serious. We have to be careful what we say.

Johann   Or?

Carl   All sorts of things. Father, listen. People disappear. They –

Johann   Who disappeared?

He has stopped eating. He pushes his plate away. **Carl** *talks rapidly.*

Carl   Just last month. One of his cabinet, an old soldier, Gunter Brandt, was overheard making a joke – some harmless, scurrilous remark about the King – and –

Johann   What?

Carl   His body was found in the forest. Bullet through the brain. They say he had an accident cleaning his pistol. Please! This is a man who'd fought in thirty battles – How could he make that sort of mistake? . . . and, believe me, there are others . . . not all their bodies are found . . .

Johann *nods. Speaks more quietly.*

Johann   Things in Leipzig are no better. We've had two months of it. Kessler's daughter was raped.

Carl   My God!

Johann   She can't have been the only one, but – what do you expect? Two thousand men roaming the city. Billeted in people's homes. They took over the garrison. There's been a lot of blood. Hangings and –

He pours some wine.

Carl   But why Leipzig?

Johann   Why not? He'd murdered half Silesia. Why pay for barracks when the Leipzig council can do it?

Carl   But did he lay siege to the city?

Johann   Didn't have to. The council surrendered. The moment his army came over the hill. Opened the gates, gave his troops free rein. The town became one big brothel. Overnight. One big trough. Two months later they're still there. They've left us bankrupt and – the filth! I can't describe it. So the prospect of Leipzig's cantor paying homage to Prussia's monarch may not bring a smile to my burgher's lips.

Carl   Well, they should pay you properly. Then you wouldn't seek the patronage of a monarch you –

Johann   Despise?

Carl   Stop!

There is a knock at the door. In spite of himself, **Carl** *jumps.*

Carl   Come in.

Graun *enters apologetically.*

Graun   Forgive my intrusion. I left something on the clavier.

Carl   Please.

Graun *scuttles to the clavier and removes a piece of manuscript from the music rest.*

Graun   My apologies. I thought it better I come now than when you might be sleeping.

Johann   That's very considerate, Herr Graun. Goodnight.

Graun   Goodnight, Herr Bach. I hope you sleep well.

He exits.

Johann   The council will see me as a traitor. A Prussian crawler.

He pours some more wine.

So what? They hate me whatever I do.

Carl   I thought things were better.

Johann   They were. Briefly. Now it's back to normal. They hinder my every move, criticise everything I do. I work eighteen hours a day and get no thanks. They expect a new cantata every Sunday. I start it on Monday, finish late on Tuesday, if I'm quick – begin copying the parts, which, with even six people working flat out, can take two days, – rehearse the singers, rehearse the musicians – I'm responsible for four churches now – inspect the organs, the claviers, rehearse the boys; compose for funerals, compose for weddings, compose for executions – and that's all before Sunday, when I'm in the church at dawn, praying there'll be time to go through any changes.

A beat.

And here? How are things? Since your promotion?

Carl   I could do with a better salary. I submitted a request but he sent it back with 'no' in the margin.

Johann   So what keeps you here?

Carl   Good question. I have debts –

Johann   Big?

Carl   A few thousand.

That's a lot! **Johann** *whistles.*

Carl   – And I have children now. The thought of hawking my wares around the courts of Europe makes me weary. Also, I enjoy my fellow musicians – even though they all earn treble my wage.

Johann   Treble?

Carl   I earn three hundred thaler a year. I know for a fact that Quantz gets nearly two thousand.

Johann *puts his head in his hands.*

Carl   The other two – Graun and Benda – probably get something similar. So –

He makes a helpless gesture.

Johann   Quantz, Graun and Benda. They sound like a firm of bent lawyers.

Carl *laughs.*

Carl   I'll tell them you said that. It's not as though my presence would be greatly missed.

The King likes my music – or says he does – but I think it often confuses him. And he can never quite manage the rhythmic challenges. He prefers to play Graun or Quantz or –

Johann   The bent lawyers.

Carl   Exactly. So what leverage do I have?

Johann   Not much. I told you about Kessler, didn't I?

Carl *frowns. This again?*

Carl   His daughter. Yes. What happened?

Johann *shakes his head, unable to go there. He rubs his eyes.*

Carl   Are your eyes sore?

Johann   And itchy. I had them examined a few days back by an oculist. John Taylor. He's English. Travels in a scarlet coach covered with painted eyes.

Carl   How modest.

Johann   Said my urine tasted sweet.

Carl   What does that mean?

Johann   No idea.

Carl   I hope he didn't put it in your eyes.

Johann   He's going to operate. When I get home.

Carl   Be careful.

Johann   They say he treated Handel. Without surgery, he says I'll be blind in a year.

Carl   And with it, you could be blind in a day.

Johann   I'm in God's hands.

Carl   True. His and John Taylor's. Eat!

He pushes the plate closer to his father.

Scene Three

A room in the palace.

The room serves as a general music studio and store room. Some of the many shelves are piled with scores, others hold a variety of wind instruments plus a small drum. A couple of violins hang on the wall and a cello is propped in the corner. There is a lot of manuscript paper on the floor.

Quantz *sits on a chair.*

The door opens and **Graun** *enters. He waves the piece of manuscript paper triumphantly in the air.*

Quantz   Ah!

Graun   Luckily he hadn't seen it!

He places the piece of manuscript paper on the harpsichord's music rest. **Quantz** *gazes at it.*

Benda *comes over to the harpsichord and stares at the music. Plays it through. Ten notes. Shakes his head –*

Benda   I'm not quite sure what we're doing.

Graun   That's because you don't listen! We're attempting to make this impossible –

Benda   Impossible?

Graun   To develop into a fugue.

Benda   I see. Why are we doing that?

Graun   Because His Majesty wants to confound old Bach.

Benda   Why?

Quantz   It's a joke.

Benda   I see. What's funny about it?

Quantz   Nothing. The King wants to present Herr Bach with this theme, ask him to improvise a fugue on it – and then watch him flounder.

Benda   Why?

Quantz   No idea. Graun?

Graun *shrugs.*

Benda   But why?

Quantz   Is that the only word you know?

Benda   I'm in the middle of a concerto, I'm teaching, I have two concerts next week. I really don't have time for party games!

Quantz   Fine.

Graun   You're not the only person with work to do, Franz. I'm weeks behind with a set of trios –

Quantz   As am I, with two new sonatas. Fritz never stops asking for them. However –

Graun   We're meeting him in the morning, and I for one have no wish to turn up empty-handed.

Quantz   That can't happen.

Graun   Unthinkable.

Quantz   So? In or out?

Benda *sighs wearily.* **Emelia** *enters, carrying a tray with wine and a pot of coffee.* **Benda** *plays the theme through slowly. It hangs in the air.*

Benda   It's original. I'll give it that. Who wrote it?

Quantz/Graun   The King!

Benda   Oh my God!

He plays it again. **Emelia** *pours coffee into three cups and listens to the composers chat with some interest.*

Graun   I tried to improvise a fugue on it this morning –

Benda   Any luck?

Graun   Well, improvising fugues is hardly my forte, but I didn't get very far.

Benda   Hard to see how you could. It's so chromatic and –

Graun   Irregular. It's too long. Too clumsy.

Quantz   True – but I like its solemnity.

Graun   Yes, it has a strange, sad haughtiness –

Benda   Like its creator.

Quantz   Shhh!

Graun   But, in the end, it was pretty much – unfuguable.

Laughter.

Benda   Unfuguable! Brilliant! Unfuguable!

Emelia *leaves.* **Quantz** *gets himself a cup of coffee.*

Quantz   Very good, Graun. However, 'unfuguable' as it may be, we need to make it even more so. That's our brief.

Benda   Ridiculous!

Quantz   Possibly. And the sooner we do that, the better.

Graun   Agreed

Quantz   So let's get on with it.

They all stare at the manuscript.

Quantz   All suggestions welcome.

They continue to stare. Nobody speaks – as the lights fade.

Scene Four

The palace. **Johann**'s *room (as before).*

Johann *is sitting on a chair, staring thoughtfully at the large portrait of Friedrich Wilhelm. He walks to the portrait. Stands beneath it.*

Johann   That's the King's father, isn't it? Friedrich Wilhelm.

Carl   It is.

Johann *stares up at it.*

Johann   Looks like a pig.

Carl *laughs.*

Carl   I can't believe I'm hearing this.

Johann   Don't you think? A pig in a suit. He collected giants. Did you know that? He scoured Prussia for the tallest men and offered them cash to join his army.

Carl   I know. When I first arrived here, some of them were still on parade. Two of them were over seven feet tall.

Johann   And no sooner does this lunatic die than his son drops his flute and marches on Silesia. Nobody knows how many were killed. Nobody has any idea.

Carl   So what! It's nothing to do with us.

Johann   I've seen how his men behave – and that was just billets. Christ knows how they acted in a war. There are great pits. That's what they say. Vast pits filled with rotting dead.

Carl   Who told you this?

Johann   On Easter Sunday, some of his soldiers attended mass at the Thomaskirche. They filled ten pews. But there was one of them sat on his own. I spotted him in the organ mirror. A boy of about sixteen. Several pews back. Pressed against the wall. Small, nondescript, spotty, his whole body shaking inside his uniform. Mouthing on his own. I saw him drop his Bible and scramble to the floor like a field mouse. There was nothing of him. When the service finished he stayed in his pew, mumbling prayers and weeping. I waited till the church was empty and I walked up the aisle to his –

The memory stops him.

He looked – he was – so frail – so –

He pulls himself together.

I sat next to him, tried to find out who he was, but he stammered badly. All he could talk about were pits. Blood-smeared grass. Body parts. Birds pecking dead children. He asked if that would be hell. Was hell like that?

*He catches **Carl**'s concerned expression – and suddenly realises how all this must sound. He shakes his head and attempts a smile. Shrugs.*

Johann   I know. I'm not at my best –

Carl   You seem somewhat – troubled. Preoccupied.

Johann *laughs.*

Johann   True! It's a paradox but – as my eyes get worse I seem to see more clearly. 'For now, we see through a glass, darkly.'

A beat.

I wake earlier and earlier and I lie there – staring into the dark. Sometimes it's three in the morning. I go to my desk, light a candle – sit listening to my family sleeping. By nine I'm exhausted.

A beat.

You're right. I am preoccupied.

Carl   With what?

Johann   With – well – recently I've become more and more –

Carl   What?

He shakes his head.

Johann   I'm not talking about anything obscure. It's real, it's solid. It just sounds so strange when I try to –

He struggles for the right words.

It's – it's the moment – the moment when one thing becomes another. When –

Carl   I'm sorry. When one thing –?

Johann   There – you see! I told you – it's –

Carl   No. Go on!

Johann   The myriad possibilities open in that tiny fraction of time and the – Alright. A mundane example. Suppose you want to pick up that pen.

Carl   Yes?

Johann   So. Go on. Do it.

Carl *picks up the quill pen.*

Johann   Alright. Now break down the steps. There's the want, the need, the desire to pick it up – yes? Then, from that want comes the decision to take it – and from that decision comes the action, the movement, the grasping, the picking up.

Carl   Aha?

Johann   But, between the two – between the want and the action – there's a tiny moment – a moment so blurred, so grey, so fragile, you'd never be able to locate it – but it's there nonetheless. A fraction of a fraction of a second in which the want becomes a decision, and the decision becomes a deed.

Carl *laughs in exasperation.*

Carl   So why are you so –?

Johann   Because, because within that tiny moment of grey – inside that dark, fraction-of-a-fraction of a second, lies the possibility of –

He struggles to explain.

Something else.

Carl   Something else?

Johann *becomes increasingly frustrated.*

Johann   Yes!

Carl   What? What else?

Johann   I don't know! That's the point! I don't know!

He swallows the wine.

What I do know is that each new day reconfirms our genius for terror! Doesn't it? Every act of kindness, every act of charity, every act of love is matched ten-fold by some new obscenity – some dreadful testimony to our inevitable damnation.

Carl *is trying to follow.*

Carl   Well – I could equally say – every act of terror is matched by ten acts of love. How could you prove otherwise?

Johann   Carl, this isn't a student debate!

Carl   I never thought it was – I'm just saying – what's any of this to do with the grey moment between impulse –

Johann   – And action? Because – because it's the moment of divine intervention! Don't you see? It has to be! That's it!

Carl   I see. Well –

Johann   God's purpose. One moment, there's nothing. Then, there's something! Your mind's blank – then there's an idea. From second to second! There it is. The germ of your cantata, your chorale, your partita. Out of the void. Out of nothing – to something. In a millionth of a second! A divine spark.

There is a knock on the door. Both men jump. **Carl** *stands.*

Carl   Come in.

Emelia *enters.* **Carl** *grins.*

Carl   Oh. I thought you might be an angel.

Emelia   No such luck, dear. And for your further disappointment, Herr von Meckelsdorf has asked if he may speak to you for a moment.

Carl   I shall come at once. This will only take a few minutes, Father –

He moves towards the door. **Johann** *waves a dismissive hand.*

Emelia   And you have a visitor, Herr Bach.

A slim and extremely smartly dressed man sweeps into the room. **Emelia** *announces him.*

Emelia   Herr Voltaire.

Voltaire *bows low.* **Johann** *returns the bow – as does* **Carl**.

Voltaire   Herr Bach, I beg you to forgive my intrusion.

Johann   Monsieur Voltaire, no intrusion could please me more. This is indeed a great honour.

Voltaire   Herr Bach – the honour is entirely mine. Believe me.

Carl   Will you excuse me, monsieur? I was just on my way to see Herr von Meckelsdorf and –

Voltaire   Please! Please!

The two men bow to each other and **Carl** *leaves with* **Emelia**. **Voltaire** *turns back to* **Johann**.

Voltaire   Ten minutes ago, Herr Bach, I was in my carriage! On alighting, I was fortunate enough to collide with Emelia, who told me of your arrival. I have not even changed my coat –

Johann   Again – I am more than deeply honoured, monsieur –

Voltaire *waves* **Johann**'s *words away.*

Voltaire   Please! But, I must beseech your complicity in *une petite deception*. His Majesty gives a concert – even as we speak – a concert at which I should be present but –

He shrugs philosophically.

Since I am already late I thought perhaps there could be no harm in paying my respects to you, Herr Bach, before I go to the hall.

But you have not seen me!

Johann   I shall not breathe a word of this encounter. You have my word. If we see each other again it will be as if for the first time.

Voltaire *makes a little bow.*

Voltaire   *Vous-êtes galant*, monsieur. How long are you at court?

Johann   Three, four days.

Voltaire *steps back with a display of Gallic disappointment.*

Voltaire   *Non*! *Seulement*? *Je suis désolé*!

Johann   And you?

Voltaire   *Qui sait*?

Johann   Then I pray we will find time to speak at length, monsieur.

Voltaire   That wish will crown my orisons, Herr Bach. No words can express my reverence for your music. *Mais* –

His tone becomes conspiratorial.

Voltaire   *Soyez très prudent. Ici. Soyez sur vos gardes*!

Voltaire *looks at him with great meaning.* **Johann** *is confused. His French is bad.*

Johann   *Pourquoi*, monsieur?

Johann   *Les trucs. Les pièges.*

He raises a meaningful finger. **Johann** *is none the wiser.*

A cannon fires somewhere nearby. Both men acknowledge the explosion. **Voltaire** *gives a wry smile.*

Voltaire   Prussia is not a state in possession of an army. It is an army in possession of a state. I say no more.

He places a finger over his lips.

Voltaire   *Pour vous seul. Vous comprenez?*

Johann *nods mystified.*

Voltaire   And now – I must hurry. I already languish in a somewhat ambivalent favour here. I have no wish to exacerbate that condition.

Johann   And I no desire to be its cause, monsieur.

They laugh.

Voltaire   *À bientôt*, Herr Bach.

They bow to each other and **Voltaire** *leaves with a wave as* **Carl** *enters again. The two men bow to each other in passing.*

Carl   You're honoured indeed!

Johann   What's he doing here?

Carl   Good question. He's been at court several months. Quite why remains a mystery. He and the King are very close. They spend hours together. Walking, dining – talking. Always talking.

A beat.

There are all sorts of rumours.

Johann   About what?

Carl *shakes his head.*

Johann   What sort of rumours?

Carl   They think he's a spy.

Johann   For France?

Carl   Of course. And they may be right. How do I know? What was he saying to you?

Johann   No idea. It was all in French. But he seems nervous. Like you. 'Don't say this and don't say that! I'm not really here. You haven't seen me. I haven't even seen myself!' What's the matter with you all?

Carl   Try working here.

Johann   Voltaire's an atheist isn't he?

Carl *is taken aback by the suddenness of this question.*

Carl   An atheist?

Johann   That's what I heard.

Carl *shrugs.* **Johann** *stares at him.*

Carl   Herr von Meckelsdorf asked me to give you this.

Johann   Who's he?

Carl   Secretary to His Majesty.

He hands **Johann** *the file and the envelope.* **Emelia** *enters. She moves towards the table and looks at the half-eaten food.*

Emelia   Have you finished eating, sir, or –?

Johann   Thank you – yes. But please leave the wine and some –

Emelia   – glasses. I will indeed, sir.

She puts the remaining food, the plates and cutlery onto a tray – whilst **Johann** *opens the envelope, pulls out a letter and reads.*

Carl   Anything interesting?

Johann   Letter of welcome – and my itinerary for the next three days.

He skims the letter. He suddenly looks up, throws the letter onto the table.

Johann   When do I meet the King?

Carl   The King is elusive. Sometimes he –

Johann   He's playing in a concert!

Carl   Study your itinerary. Drink some wine. Have a rest.

He gets up and pours some more wine – hands the glass to **Johann***, who drinks it in one draught.* **Carl** *watches, slightly concerned.*

Johann   What are the King's beliefs?

Carl   I don't think he has any.

Johann *goes to the bottle and refills his glass.*

Carl   Why don't you get undressed and I'll –

Johann   Carl! Listen to me!

He sits heavily at the table.

Johann   I'm sixty-two.

Carl   I know.

Johann   I can't sleep. My eyes are terrible, I have digestive problems. I worry –

Carl   Would you like to see a doctor?

Johann   Absolutely not!

Carl   Because there are several physicians in the court and –

Johann   No. I don't want that. Carl, listen. There are six words that have been the guiding tenet of my life –

He bangs his fist silently on the table with each word.

I. Know. That. My. Redeemer. Liveth.

Carl *takes a deep breath.*

Carl   Father, look –

Johann   And – the extraordinary power –

Carl   I think you should –

Johann   – the stupendous gift with which God has blessed me has been dedicated entirely to celebrating that knowledge. Nothing else. Well, what else is there? But, as my eyesight dims and my end approaches, I grow daily less assured of our salvation.

Carl   Salvation?

Johann *gets up.*

Johann   For God's sake! What kind of redemption's feasible when bishops lead children into battle and priests bless the butchered dead? As though –

Carl   This is pretty old ground. Isn't it?

Johann   Not to me.

Carl   Really? Really? Name me a time when it was any different. And what's any of that to do with your quandary over accepting Fritz's invitation?

Johann   Whose invitation?

Carl   Oh – I'm sorry. That's the nickname we give His Majesty. Behind his back. The whole court does it. It's become second nature. We call him Fritz.

Johann   I could think of some better names.

Carl   But do you really feel you've forfeited redemption?

Johann *shrugs.*

Carl   That God will judge you? For what? Coming to Potsdam?

Johann   Or for not coming. He will judge my motives.

Johann *struggles with this and then just shakes his head.*

Carl   So, God told you to come?

Johann *shrugs helplessly.*

Johann   He'll reveal why. In time. He always does.

Carl   In which case, why should He judge your motive for accepting the invitation?

Johann *wrestles with this for a moment.*

Johann   I'm a musician. I play. People listen. But what if I know that one of my listeners has killed – not just one person – but thousands? What then?

Carl   Father, for God's sake! He's the King of Prussia! He fights wars!

Johann   And he murders civilians. His soldiers rape civilians.

A long moment. Then **Johann** *puts his face in his hands.* **Carl** *watches him, not sure what to do.*

Carl   Are you alright?

Johann   No.

He gets up and goes to the window. Struggles to open it.

How does this thing open?

Carl *walks over and fiddles with the window catch. Opens it.* **Johann** *breathes the air deeply. An explosion is heard in the distance.*

Johann   I'm sorry, Carl. I've become terrible company. I never meant to start this conversation. It's just that –

Carl   I understand.

Johann *sits.*

Carl   Why don't you undress?

Johann *nods. He gets up and, aided by* **Carl***, begins to remove his clothes. They talk as he does so.*

Johann   Do you have to work tomorrow?

Carl   Yes. I have an orchestra rehearsal at nine – and then I must spend the morning finishing a flute concerto for His Majesty.

Johann *struggles with his jacket.*

Johann   I think you are an extraordinary composer.

Carl *is taken completely off guard.*

Johann   I mean it. You know I don't give praise for the sake of it.

Carl *smiles. Touched.*

Carl   I wish my employer felt the same.

Johann   He doesn't?

Carl   He's a reasonable flautist but his tastes never move. I'd say he was traditional. Conservative. He likes his music straightforward, predictable . . . pretty . . .

Johann   Can you reach this button?

Carl *undoes a button at the back of* **Johann***'s breeches.*

Johann   How many keyboards does he have?

Carl   Several. Mainly harpsichords.

Johann   Any good?

Carl   I think so.

Johann *indicates the file.*

Johann   He's asked me to inspect them all. And the organ in –

Carl   The Garrison Church?

Johann *nods. He takes his breeches off and stands bare-legged in his shirt.*

Johann   I didn't bring a nightshirt.

Carl   I can get you anything you need.

Johann *wanders over to the clavichord in his shirt. He opens the lid. Sits and stares at the label above the keys. Beams.*

Johann   Ah – Silbermann!

Carl   They're all Silbermann. Mostly harpsichords. I think this is the only clavier.

Johann   I was with him last week. Silbermann.

Carl   Is he well?

Johann   Not bad. He has eye problems.

Carl   You could see Taylor together.

Johann *plays a chord followed by a flurry of notes. Nods approvingly.*

Johann   Nice sound but – something's flat? The middle D?

Plays rapid chromatic scales.

Johann   Do you still have your Silbermann clavier?

Carl *shakes his head sadly.*

Carl   I had to sell it. Last year.

Johann   Your king doesn't put his hand in his pocket, does he?

Carl   Play something. Come on.

Johann *takes off his wig, scratches his head vigorously, throws the wig to one side and starts to play an extremely complex and dazzling prelude, his head bent low over the keys.*

The prelude builds in both intensity and volume. **Carl** *listens, rapt in admiration. Suddenly –*

The door swings open and **King Frederick** *sweeps into the room followed by* **Voltaire** *and a flurry of courtiers. Two of the courtiers carry lighted candelabras. All at once, the room is very crowded and very bright!*

Carl *bows low, as* **Johann** *jumps to his feet in alarm.*

Johann   Majesty!

Frederick *gestures to* **Johann** *to continue playing. Somewhat flustered,* **Johann** *sits back down and resumes the prelude. As the music continues –*

Frederick *moves a little closer to the harpsichord and watches* **Johann** *with genuine fascination. The courtiers spread out and assume listening postures.* **Voltaire** *stands rooted to the spot.*

With a flourish, **Johann** *manages to bring the prelude to an early close. Everyone applauds enthusiastically and* **Johann** *stands and gives a little bow – but then, suddenly, and too late, remembering his state of undress, he attempts to cover himself.* **Frederick** *laughs – and the courtiers all smile.*

Johann   I'm – Oh my God! –

Frederick   Please! Herr Bach! It is I who must apologise. I entered entirely unannounced. But who could resist such beauty? Bravo! *Magnifique*! *Magnifique*!

Voltaire   Bravo! Superb! (*Etc.*)

More applause from the room, as **Carl** *throws* **Johann** *his breeches.* **Johann** *scrambles to put them on, while at the same time grabbing his wig and placing it on his head, slightly askew. Chaotic and red-faced he attempts to speak . . .*

Johann   Majesty – had I even the slightest inkling that –

Frederick   I'm a soldier, Herr Bach. I assure you this is not the first time I've seen a man with no trousers.

Johann   Of course, Highness but –

Frederick   Please don't give it another thought. Ten minutes ago I was standing, flute in hand, before a splendid gathering, waiting to enchant them with one of your son's magnificent concertos –

He turns to **Carl**, *his right hand over his heart.*

Frederick   The A minor! Ah! I can't tell you how it moves me! Such pain, such grace, such acceptance, such – I don't know! Such everything! –

Back to **Johann**.

Frederick   – When my secretary informed me you had arrived. Without further ado, I stopped the orchestra and came straight here. I am honoured and entranced that you should visit my palace, Herr Bach. Honoured and entranced. And I look forward immensely to spending time with you – talking, eating, perhaps drinking a little, showing you my instruments and – above all – hearing you play.

He presents **Voltaire**, *who bows elegantly.*

Frederick   Allow me to present my dear friend Monsieur Voltaire. You have, no doubt, met before?

Johann   Never Majesty. But it is an honour –

Frederick   We have much to share with you. Much to share. We meet tomorrow. Rest well. I bid you a very good night.

He clicks his heels and nods his head. **Johann** *bows low as does* **Carl**. **Frederick** *turns and leaves the room, followed by his courtiers.* **Voltaire** *gives* **Johann** *a little smile:*

Voltaire   *Formidable*, monsieur. *Vraiment!*

He bows and leaves. With the room finally empty, **Johann** *turns on* **Carl** *in fury.*

Johann   Why didn't you say something!?

Carl   Say something? I had no idea he was coming. I'm not a clairvoyant!

Johann   I am so humiliated! So humiliated!

Carl   I really don't think –

Johann   What? What don't you really think? That this wasn't an appalling embarrassment? That this monster should discover me like some –

Carl   Calling him a monster is unhelpful! And, I should point out, dangerous!

Johann   Naked! Standing naked before the King of Prussia!

Carl   You weren't naked!

Johann   It's like everyone's worst nightmare. 'I dreamt the King of Prussia asked me to play and suddenly I was wearing no trousers.'

Carl *laughs and pulls the bell cord.*

Johann   It's not funny! How can I face him now?

Carl   Don't be ridiculous!

Johann   I shall be the laughing stock of Potsdam! The whole court will know of it!

Carl   Rubbish! What the court will know is that on the brink of making his solo flute entrance, the King of all Prussia stopped an orchestra in full flight, so that he may welcome a cantor from Saxony. Can't you see? He holds you in the highest esteem – a validation which you hardly reciprocate. Your trousers come a rather poor second.

The door opens and **Emelia** *appears.*

Carl   Please unpack Herr Bach's bags.

Emelia   Of course sir.

Johann   You can leave the smaller one. The one full of papers.

Emelia *begins to unpack* **Johann**'*s bags.*

Carl   And can you find someone to attend to my father's wig?

Emelia   Yes, sir.

Johann   What's wrong with my wig?

Carl   It's been rather thrown around and it could do with some attention. They are quite excellent here. Don't you think mine's rather fine?

Johann *removes his own wig and peruses his son's.*

Johann   How often do you have it dressed?

Carl   Most days.

Carl   Most days?!

Carl   Father – this is a royal court! It's how things are done here!

Emelia *holds out her hand and* **Johann** *gives her the wig.*

Emelia   You'll have this back first thing tomorrow, sir.

Johann   Have you worked here long?

Emelia   Fifty years, sir.

Johann   Fifty years! I see. So you worked for the old king? Friedrich Wilhelm!

Carl *takes a sharp intake of breath and gives his father a 'proceed with care' look.*

Emelia   Ah! I was one of his chambermaids. Two years. And my husband was his valet.

Johann   Ah! So you saw –

Emelia   Enough to last me three lifetimes.

They all laugh.

But I'll say this, Herr Bach –

She approaches **Johann**, *a pair of stockings still dangling from her hand.*

Emelia   – Because I'm sure I'll never get another chance. I was in Leipzig – must be four, five years ago – visiting my sister. She works in the church –

Johann   Which one?

Emelia   With the white tower . . .

Johann   St Thomas?

Emelia   That's it.

Johann   What's your sister's name?

Emelia   Ulrike. Ulrike Köchner.

Johann   Ulrike! I know her very well. She cleans the pews and –

Emelia   Her husband looks after the building –

Johann   He's the caretaker. Tall with a big moustache. Gustav!

Emelia   Gustav. And Ulrike took me there on Good Friday. We weren't standing. You'd reserved her two places. We were sitting in a pew, halfway up . . . I tell you, Herr Bach.

The sunshine came pouring through those big windows! It dazzled me! The walls all white – and the golden pipes! And two orchestras! One on each side. Two orchestras. In a church . . .

Johann   When was this? Forty-two?

Emelia   It was five years ago so – yes. Forty-two. Easter forty-two.

Johann   My St Matthew. My Matthew Passion.

Emelia   Ah –

Johann   April forty-two. Its third performance. I'd made some changes, – you were lucky!

Carl   I was at the first performance, Emelia. I was thirteen.

Emelia *turns to* **Carl**.

Emelia   Then you'll know. I tell you, sir – if I never hear anything else.

Back to **Johann**.

Emelia   St Matthew! My God! And the choir – the singers – I never heard anything like it! Never. And, you won't believe this – when they were walking Him to Golgotha, a bird flew into the church. It fluttered onto a beam, high up over the altar. And when they'd crucified Him it flew away. That's the truth. I saw it.

The memory stops her.

Sometimes I stop. Even now. I just stop and I remember sitting in that church . . . never knew there was such beauty in the world, Herr Bach.

The old woman bows low. **Johann** *takes her hands and brings her up.*

Johann   Thank you. Thank you.

Emelia   I'll put your stockings in your bedroom.

She takes a bunch more stockings from **Johann***'s bag and disappears into the bedroom.* **Johann** *moves towards the bedroom and continues conversing with her while she's inside.*

Johann   So. The old king? Was he good to you?

Emelia (*off stage*)   Not very. Too free with his stick.

Johann   He beat you?

Emelia (*off stage*)   No. But he beat everybody else.

Carl *waves at* **Johann** *to 'leave it' but, as* **Emelia** *emerges from the bedroom,* **Johann** *continues, unfazed. He refers to the picture while he talks.*

Johann   And was he good to his son?

Carl *gives* **Johann** *another 'don't go there' intake of breath. The old woman looks quizzically at* **Johann**.

Emelia   Herr Bach – do you have sons?

Johann   I've had eleven. This is one of them.

Emelia *makes a little bow to* **Carl** *who nods back.*

Emelia   And we're very proud of him here, Herr Bach. Very proud.

Carl   Thank you, Emelia.

Emelia   Only telling the truth, sir. Well, the old king had three. Three sons. They were all terrified. Kept out of his way.

Carl   Didn't he fire a gun outside their window . . .?

Emelia   Not a gun – a cannon! To wake them up. That's right. Every morning. Five o'clock. Bang! Imagine . . .

Johann   I'd rather not! But, tell me, was he good to little Frederick?

Emelia   You don't want to know. He beat him. Beat him for anything and everything . . . Falling off his horse, wearing gloves, not wearing gloves, forgetting his Latin, playing his flute.

Carl   That's what I heard from Gunter Brandt. He said Frederick was forced into the cadets.

Emelia   To make a man of him.

Carl   He saw the King drag his seventeen-year-old son across the parade ground.

Emelia   I couldn't look. Kicking him! Kicking him. In front of everybody!

Carl   The whole regiment at attention. Eyes front. The rain pouring down. No wonder the boy ran away –

Emelia   That's right! With a friend. Fellow officer. Rumour had it they were trying to get to England. But someone spilled the beans and they were arrested.

Johann   What happened?

Emelia   Don't ask. His Majesty was like a man on fire! Screaming, foaming, black in the face. He charged them with treason. Yes. Treason! For doing what?

Carl   They locked the prince in a cell.

Johann   How long was he there?

Emelia   Three months. And when he got out the King had him working in the War Departments. Learning all about war.

Johann   But, tell me – the prince's friend? The one he ran away with?

Emelia   Hermann Katte.

Johann   Yes. What happened to him?

Emelia   They cut his head off.

Johann *stares at her in horror.*

Emelia   I heard it from a soldier who was there. In Kustrin. They made the prince watch. Dragged him to his cell window. Made him look through the bars.

A beat.

They say he never mentioned Katte's name again. They say he abandoned all faith. Refused a Bible, refused a prayer book, wouldn't talk to a priest. And I believe them. He's never in church.

Johann   I'm meeting him in a church tomorrow. How long before his father died?

Emelia   Too long. Oh, by the way, I've been meaning to ask –

A bell rings somewhere outside. **Emelia** *starts towards the door, picking up* **Johann***'s wig on the way.*

Emelia   That'll be for me! Anything you want, Herr Bach – just ring.

She turns at the door.

The day the old king died, my husband took me in his arms and we danced. I don't know which of us was the happier.

She exits. **Johann** *laughs.*

Johann   She's a walking scandal sheet! How come she wasn't shot in the woods long ago!

Carl   There's still time. She's been here so long she's part of the furniture. Maybe it's earned her a form of exemption! And then she's got a soft spot for you. But the thing to remember is – we heard none of it.

Johann   Never happened.

Carl   Absolutely! And tomorrow – whatever happens – and whatever's said –

Johann   Keep smiling. I understand. Dolce, piano, legato, sotto voce –

Carl   Promise?

Johann   You have my word –

Emelia *re-enters. She stands in the doorway.*

Emelia   Herr Bach? I wanted to ask – what's a fugue? They say you're famous for them. Fugues. I was wondering what they are.

Johann *and* **Carl** *look at each other. How to even begin?*

Johann   Come to the Garrison Church tomorrow and I'll play you one.

Emelia *grins.*

Emelia   I will. Thank you.

And she leaves.

Johann   She's a force of nature!

Carl *extends a hand to his father.*

Carl   Come on. Bedtime.

Johann *allows himself to be pulled to his feet.*

Carl   Big day tomorrow.

Blackout.

Act Two

Scene One

Afternoon. The Bach apartment.

Anna *sits writing. Her table is strewn with papers. Choral singing wafts from a rehearsal somewhere below. A maid enters followed by a sergeant of the Prussian Army.*

Anna *looks up. The sergeant approaches. His face is scarred and he needs a shave.*

Helstein   I counted fifty beds up there.

Anna   Exactly. There are fifty boys in the school.

Helstein   But I noticed some gaps. I was thinking –

Anna   Yes?

Helstein   Well, I'm only after accomodation for six – maybe, seven men –

Anna   Sergeant Helstein, if I'm correct, you spoke to my husband a few months ago.

Helstein   Is he here?

Anna   If he was you'd be speaking to him. But I can assure you – our situation hasn't changed. I think Herr Bach made it very clear. We are unable to billet any soldiers in this building.

Helstein   That was then. This is now. Our ranks have swollen. There's a lot of men been transferred over from Sellerhausen and they need quarters. There's room up there for at least ten.

Anna   I don't want that. This is a school. The boys work very hard and they need to sleep. I don't want –

Helstein   What you want and what you'll get are two very different things, Frau Bach.

A beat.

Anna   Are you threatening me?

Helstein   I'm telling you.

Anna   I see. And what happens if I refuse?

Helstein   I think that would be foolish.

Anna   That's not really an answer, is it?

Helstein   Call it what you like –

Anna   Because I doubt very much that you've got the authority to enforce this issue, Sergeant –

Helstein   Jesus! You people! Don't tell me what I've got and what I haven't got. Get that attic ready – and if you need to kick a few boys out – just do it.

He takes a step towards her.

Anna   Please understand, I will be registering a complaint.

Helstein   Oh really? I'm shaking in my boots! A complaint? Who to?

Anna *picks up a document. A wax seal dangles from the end of the page. White with anger, she stands and brandishes the letter at the sergeant. As he looks, his face begins to pale.*

Anna   That's right, it's from your commander-in-chief, King Frederick. If you read it you will see that it's an invitation to visit him in Potsdam. My husband accepted and he's there at this very moment. A coach leaves here this evening with some music and documents requested by your monarch – and, unless you vacate my home by the time I count to ten, Sergeant Helstein, I can assure you that my letter to King Frederick, specifying your name, your rank and your regiment, will be included in that bundle.

The sergeant stares at her in dumb fury. After a moment **Anna** *begins to count slowly.*

Anna   One . . . two . . . three . . .

The sergeant clicks his heels and leaves, slamming the door behind him. **Anna** *sits back shakily onto her chair.*

Downstairs the boys are still singing.

Scene Two

Early morning. Potsdam. A hall in the palace. Brilliant spring sunshine pours through the windows. **Carl** *sits at a harpsichord playing one of his own compositions – a complex, quirky piece.*

Frederick *enters unseen. Stands listening.* **Carl** *finishes.*

Frederick   Bravo! *Mon cher* Charles! Bravo!

Carl *jumps up.*

Frederick   What is that?

Carl   My toccata, Your Highness.

Frederick   In?

Carl   C minor.

Frederick   Wonderful! *Je l'adore!* Heaven! We must have this at Friday's concert.

Carl   Of course.

Frederick   How is your father this morning?

Carl   I haven't yet seen him, Your Highness. He was extremely tired last night . . .

Frederick   Of course. He must sleep. Not everyone keeps my hours. What time is it now?

Carl   Seven thirty, Majesty.

Frederick   Let him rest. I have prepared a long day for him.

Quantz, **Benda** *and* **Graun** *enter. They are all dressed in their finest clothes.*

Frederick   Ah! Quantz! Benda! Graun! You come most carefully upon your hour.

They all bow. **Quantz** *produces a piece of manuscript paper. It has a single line of notes written on it.*

Benda   We have been quite industrious, Your Highness.

Graun   Never did three composers work harder on twenty notes . . .

Quantz   But we believe, sire, that we have now honed your masterpiece to a devilish perfection.

Frederick *rubs his hands with excitement.* **Quantz** *gives it to him.*

Quantz   It must be said at once, Majesty, that, try as we might, none of us was able to improvise a fugue on your extraordinary theme.

Graun   And, oh how we tried!

Benda   Impossible! Unfuguable!

Quantz   Yes, in its virgin state, and without any tinkering by us, the theme presents an almost insurmountable harmonic challenge. It is extremely original –

Benda   Unique, in my opinion –

Quantz   – and, distinguished of course, by its extreme chromaticism. However, in searching for ways that might add to its complexity, we chose to look instead at the remarkable steadiness of its *rhythmic* structure –

Graun   Which is, of course, one of its key attributes –

Quantz   And we did observe that here at the end of bar five, and here at the first beat of bar six, there is a repetition of the same note.

Benda   An E flat.

Quantz   Yes. A minim followed by a single beat. As Your Highness can see, we have tied these two notes over the bar –

Frederick   Ah!

Quantz   Thus momentarily disguising the metre –

Graun   – While leaving intact the musical integrity of your extraordinary theme. This may –

Frederick   Yes, yes, how clever. Even I can see this could pose a devilish stumbling block. Of course, I am only a humble novice at your trade –

Graun   Hardly, Your Highness!

Benda   You have a masterful grasp, sire –

Graun   Possibly the greatest flautist in Prussia!

Frederick   Sweet of you! Believe me, I know my limitations – but this is *absolument formidable*! Look what these geniuses have done, Carl!

He hands it to **Carl**.

Frederick   I gave them a theme on which old Bach could improvise a fugue, and they have disguised the metre at a crucial moment, which has provided a rhythmic snare. A musical conundrum –

Benda   In what is already an improvisor's nightmare!

Carl *quickly reads it.*

Carl   It's –

He frowns.

Quantz   Yes?

Carl *goes to the harpsichord and begins to slowly pick out the tune.*
Quantz *turns in triumph to the gleeful king.*

Quantz   Try and improvise a fugue on that!

Carl *tries and fails after a few bars.*

Quantz   Quite.

Carl   Give me pen and paper and I could –

Quantz   We could all work it out on paper, Bach. The challenge is to improvise a three-part fugue, at one sitting.

Carl *tries again and fails. Shakes his head.* **Frederick** *claps excitedly.*

Frederick   Congratulations, gentlemen! I am prepared to wager that old Bach will fail to improvise a three-part fugue out of this. Who will wager that he will?

The three musicians look at each other.

Graun   Majesty – we have spent several hours preparing this fiendish trap. It would be foolhardy to bet on something we know to be impossible.

Quantz   I'm afraid I agree, Your Highness. It will be amusing enough to watch the old man try.

Benda   My guess is he'll stumble around bar eight!

Frederick   How sad! No takers. Perhaps I shall find someone in the court. Or perhaps my sister would care to hazard a bet.

Benda   I hope she will be appraised of the odds beforehand, Majesty.

Frederick *laughs.*

Carl   I am prepared to wager, Your Majesty.

For a moment **Frederick** *is nonplussed.*

Frederick   Splendid!

Carl   But only if my fellow musicians agree to wager against me.

Frederick   So, to be clear! We four wager old Bach will be floored by our theme. And you wager he will be able to improvise a three-part fugue based on it?

Carl   Correct.

Frederick   Gentlemen?

Quantz   I have no wish to deprive you of your hard-earned money, Carl.

Benda   Nor I –

Graun   Nor I.

Benda   But if you are determined to throw it in our direction then –

Quantz   How can we resist?

Laughter.

Graun   How much shall we wager?

Frederick   I am prepared to venture a hundred thaler.

A slight wince from **Benda** *– but they're on safe ground so –*

Graun   Done. I'm prepared to wager that.

Benda   And I.

Quantz   And I.

A beat.

I hope you appreciate, Carl, that you will be four hundred thaler the poorer by this afternoon.

Carl   I doubt it.

Quantz   Why?

Carl   I was thinking of a different sum.

Frederick *looks irritated.*

Frederick   I see. Lower?

Carl   Higher, Majesty.

There is a shocked silence. Then –

Quantz   That's impossible!

Graun   Ridiculous!

Benda   Have you gone insane?

Quantz   Not at all.

Frederick   A thousand thaler?

Carl   Yes. You all seem convinced my father will fail to improvise a fugue on your theme – a theme for which, by the way, Majesty, I have the utmost admiration. I, on the other hand, believe he is eminently equipped to do so.

A silence.

We are, after all, dealing with the greatest musician in Europe.

A moment of disbelief and then **Quantz** *snorts.*

Quantz   Oh please!

Graun   Carl, he's a fine performer but that's just –

Benda   Ludicrous! Come, come! He's a solid enough keyboard player, an excellent cantor and a good composer but – 'the greatest composer and musician in Europe'? Frankly, that's preposterous.

Graun   I'm afraid it is, Carl. Old Bach's very much of the old school.

Carl *is uncomfortable.*

Carl   Look, gentlemen. I am quite happy not to bet at all. I thought we were playing a harmless prank. We've worked together in real fellowship for many years and – I have no desire to create any strain between us.

The three musicians are listening.

Carl   I would hate to deprive you of so much money.

Frederick   I fear, Bach, that it is they who will be depriving you.

Carl   Unlikely, Majesty – but all things are possible.

He turns back to his fellow musicians.

Please don't feel held to this wager. I completely understand if –

Quantz *struggles for a dignified way out.*

Quantz   Carl – I have no doubts whatsoever about the validity of our bet. However, I am sure we all agree that –

The three musicians more or less speak over each other:

Benda   You have wagered an extremely large sum!

Graun   Precisely. It's rather uncommon to wager such a grand amount on an escapade of this nature. Normally, I would imagine –

Quantz   – an amount equivalent to the original –

Graun   Yes. That might be more in keeping with –

Benda   – This sort of bet. After all, there are some occasions when –

Frederick*'s patience is now at an end. His voice cuts through.*

Frederick   I am prepared to wager.

Benda, **Quantz** and **Graun** *spin around in dismay. They are snookered and they know it.* **Frederick** *stands staring. Then, with hardly a moment's hesitation,* **Quantz** *performs a well-oiled, feudal volte-face.*

Quantz   And so am I. I am prepared to wager.

Frederick   A thousand thaler.

Quantz   A thousand thaler.

Frederick   Each.

A beat.

Quantz   Each.

The other two nod in miserable agreement. **Quantz** *is steely.*

Quantz   But under the strictest rules.

Carl   Of course.

Quantz   Firstly. Nobody sees that manuscript until old Bach sees it.

Carl   Agreed.

Quantz   You yourself, Carl, will have no contact with your father until after the event. No contact whatsoever.

Carl   Agreed.

Benda   And old Bach must improvise a three-part fugue – publicly. There and then.

Graun   At once. He may play the theme through a couple of times but –

Quantz   After that, he must begin the improvisation –

Graun   At once. And his fugue must follow the laws of harmony and counterpoint.

Benda   Strictly and to the letter.

Carl   Agreed. And payment of all debts will take place before sunset tomorrow.

Frederick   Agreed.

The three musicians nod grimly. **Frederick** *claps his hands in almost girlish glee.*

Frederick   This is exciting! Now, Quantz – my flute lesson. It'll need to be brief as I have much to do before I can spend time with old Bach. Come! Busy, busy, busy!

He bustles out with an unhappy **Quantz** *in tow. On his way out* **Quantz** *gestures to* **Benda** *and* **Graun** *to deal with* **Carl***.*

Benda   I'm going to get some breakfast. Care to join me, Carl?

Carl   I think I'll just go through this toccata once more, Franz. I have to play it on Friday at –

Graun   Carl, perhaps you didn't hear what he said.

Carl   I'm sorry?

Graun   He's inviting you for breakfast.

Carl   I know.

Graun   And when you've finished, he'll probably invite you for a stroll –

Benda   Until lunch. After which, you may both take a leisurely, post-prandial wander . . .

Graun   You don't leave our sight, Bach. Not till your father has failed to improvise that fugue.

Benda *beams at* **Carl**.

Benda   Coffee?

An explosion of music!

Scene Three

Potsdam. The Garrison Church.

High up in an organ loft **Johann** *puts the organ through its paces – testing every stop and pipe with a great fugue. His playing is dazzling and overpowering.*

The church is deserted except for the lone figure of **Emelia** *who stands in the centre aisle. She seems rooted to the spot and, as the complex strands of the fugue weave like waves through the church, bright shafts of sunlight circle her body.*

The music bleeds into the next scene as lights fade up on:

Scene Four

A smallish room in the palace.

Carl *sits writing music. There is sound of a key turning in a lock. Then a* **Maidservant** *enters with a tray of food and wine.* **Benda** *follows her. The* **Maidservant** *places the tray on a table and lays the food out in front of* **Carl***.*

Maidservant   I'm afraid it's gone cold. They wouldn't let me in.

She takes the tray and exits.

Benda   You must be hungry.

Carl   What time is it?

Benda   Around one. The King's lunching with your father and Voltaire. Eat something.

Carl *picks at the food and then moves fast.*

Carl   I've had enough of this!

He makes for the door. **Quantz** *and* **Graun** *enter. They have probably been listening outside – and position themselves between* **Carl** *and the door.*

Graun   Sorry, Carl – we can't risk any contact between the two of you. There's too much at stake.

Carl   Whose fault's that?

Benda   Yours.

Carl   Mine? I never wanted this idiotic bet in the first place! This whole business has got completely out of hand!

Benda   Only because you upped the stakes!

Carl   I was angry. That's why I –

Quantz   You multiplied them by ten!

Carl   Yes but I never expected anyone to take me up on it. Obviously!

Graun Really?

Carl Yes! Really! A thousand thaler is a fortune!

Graun So why bet it?

Carl For God's sake! I tried to talk you out of it –

Benda And I was willing –

Quantz So was I!

Benda But the King suddenly agreed and –

Graun You were hoisted by your own petard –

Carl – And none of you could lose face. I know. So, go to the King and tell him the bet's too big. Tell him you want to call it off. Either that or lower the stakes.

Quantz Too late. Anyway, it would make us look rather pathetic. But, hopefully, his theme will confound your father and we shall all make some money.

Carl Ah! So suddenly the bet's not so stupid?

Quantz Not if we win.

Carl There's no question of you winning!

Laughter.

Benda Why? Is the old man superhuman?

Carl Far from it, but his capabilities exceed every musician I know.

Graun My God!

Quantz Here we go . . .

Benda You Bachs! Unbelievable!

Graun Why don't you own up? You just don't like seeing papa beat.

Carl *stares at him in disbelief.*

Carl   Oh. So suddenly we're in the playground!

Quantz *mimics* **Carl** *cruelly.*

Quantz   'His capabilities exceed every musician I know.'

Carl   Does that irk you, Quantz?

Quantz   Who the hell do you think you're talking to? Do you think the three of us work for the greatest king in Europe because our abilities are less than your father's?

Carl   I work here and my abilities are less than his!

Quantz   Your father comes from another era, Carl.

Carl   He belongs to no era.

Benda *shakes his head in amazement.*

Benda   I don't believe I'm hearing this!

Carl   I'm simply speaking the truth?

Benda   Truth?

Carl   Well, if it's not the truth – what's all this about? Why the desire to confound him? Why the wickedly crafted theme?

Graun   It wasn't our theme!

Quantz   The King wrote it.

Carl   But you spent hours honing it! Hours engineering my father's humiliation!

Quantz   At the behest of the King.

Carl   I see. He says jump and you say how high!

Quantz   Oh please!

Benda   Grow up!

Carl   That's rich! There was a concerted effort to outwit my father. From all of you. You even tried to drag me into the plot. Or were you just trying to kiss the King's arse?

Benda Something you, of course, never do!

Carl I do little else and I despise myself for it – but answer my question. The King asked you to make it foolproof. Didn't he? Old Bach was coming and it seemed a brilliant ruse to bring him down to size. Would you do that if he was ordinary? Did you do it to Telemann? Or Weiss?

A beat.

He's an old man.

Quantz So you're concerned?

Carl Of course I'm concerned!

Benda Ah!

Carl Not because I'll lose!

Quantz Of course not!

Carl I'm concerned because he's unwell, I'm concerned because his sight's going, because he's exhausted, because he's hounded by the Leipzig authorities and never wanted to come here in the first place. And now there's this. It's cruel.

Quantz Oh boo-hoo!

Carl *punches* **Quantz** *hard in the mouth.* **Quantz** *falls to the floor with blood pouring down his chin. The other two musicians step back, appalled.* **Carl** *immediately regrets what he did.*

Carl I'm sorry, Quantz – I'm sorry! I lost my temper.

Quantz *staggers to his feet holding his mouth. The others try to help him but he pushes them to one side.*

Carl Quantz, please forgive me. This has all become ridiculous! We're behaving like –

But **Quantz** *is on his way and out of the door before* **Carl** *can finish the sentence.*

Benda Who's in the playground now?

He and **Graun** *turn and go.* **Benda** *turns back at the door.*

Benda   Don't worry. If his capabilities exceed every musician you know, you'll soon be four thousand thaler richer.

They stare at each other.

Benda   Eat something.

He leaves. **Carl** *follows him to the door. The lock is heard to turn.* **Carl** *pulls at the door. Hopeless.*

Scene Five

The palace. A spacious and elegant garden chamber.

One of the French windows is half open allowing a spring breeze to freshen the room.

Frederick *and* **Voltaire** *sit at a large round table sumptuously laid. The meal is more or less over, though cheese and nuts remain – with wine and liqueurs.*

Some attendants gracefully wait on their every need.

A harpsichord stands against one wall. **Johann***, his wig now splendidly dressed, is playing a complex and beautiful piece. He comes to the end. Both men applaud.*

Frederick   *Formidable, mon cher* Bach! *Formidable*!

Voltaire   *Magnifique*! *Magnifique*!

Frederick   That was ?

Johann   A concerto in the Italian style, Highness.

Frederick   Superb! Come and have some wine, Bach. I shall ask you to play again soon – if that is agreeable to you.

Johann   It would be my pleasure, Majesty.

He gets up from the harpsichord and makes his way to the table. **Frederick** *fills his glass with wine and raises his own.*

Frederick   Your very good health, Bach.

Voltaire *toasts* **Johann**.

Voltaire   It is a great honour to be with you today, Herr Bach. I salute you.

He raises his glass and **Johann** *reciprocates.*

Johann   And for me also, monsieur. This is a great –

Frederick *turns to* **Voltaire**, *picking up on a previous discussion.*

Frederick   Of course, Marville always surprises . . .

Voltaire   I agree.

Frederick   Though I could do without his wretched arm movements.

He imitates an elaborate, sideways swing. **Voltaire** *has a go too.*

Voltaire   Yes. Why does he do that?

Frederick   So much better to stand still – to move normally.

Voltaire   'Nor do not saw the air too much with your hand thus, but use all gently.' Shakespeare.

Frederick   Well, you know my views on Shakespeare!

Voltaire   I think they came from me.

Laughter.

Frederick   You must forgive us, Bach. We were resuming a discussion that we were pursuing before lunch concerning my acting company – a superb troupe from Paris. I am quite devoted to them. Do you know the plays of Shakespeare?

Johann   I have read only one, Your Majesty – and I fear it was a poor translation.

Frederick   And which was that?

Johann   It was called *Hamlet*. I read it last year.

Frederick   And?

Johann   Well, my English is almost non-existent and therefore I have no way of comparing this text with the original – but I was very struck by the immediacy of some of the ideas.

Frederick   Indeed. I've never liked this play.

Voltaire   Which ideas, Bach?

A beat.

Johann   Hamlet seemed a very remarkable young man – full of thought, full of feeling. Knowing what he knows demands action. Revenge. But the prospect of killing his uncle presents a crisis of conscience. It paralyses his will.

Voltaire   But why? His uncle was a murderer.

Frederick   Yes – precisely. Get on with it. Kill him.

Johann   Well, I suppose –

A beat.

Frederick   Yes?

Johann   I suppose some people might find that problematic.

Frederick *snorts with derision.*

Frederick   Would you find it difficult to kill your father's murderer, Bach?

Johann   I hope so, Majesty.

Frederick   But why?

Johann   God has commanded, 'Thou shalt not kill.'

Frederick   Yes, yes, yes – but doesn't He also command 'an eye for an eye, a tooth for a tooth'?

Voltaire   And in Deuteronomy – 'thine eye shall not pity; life shall go for life, eye for an eye, tooth for tooth –'

Frederick   This ghastly obsession with teeth!

A beat.

Johann   What happened to turning the other cheek?

Voltaire   Who has one left to turn?

Frederick *laughs.*

Frederick   But, I've often thought that commandment incorrectly translated. Rather than, 'thou shalt not kill', shouldn't it read '*who* shalt thou not kill'?

Voltaire *laughs nervously.*

Johann   For some, the only quandary seems to be when to stop.

Frederick   Killing?

Johann   Killing. Yes.

Voltaire   All murderers are punished – unless they kill in large numbers and to the sound of trumpets.

An awkward moment. Then the door opens and **Graun**, **Quantz** *and* **Benda** *enter.* **Quantz** *holds a handkerchief to his bloodied mouth. They bow to* **Frederick** *who rises from his chair to greet them.*

Frederick   Ah! Gentlemen! What perfect timing! Quantz are you ill? There's blood on that napkin.

Quantz   Highness – I have a cut from shaving. I apologise.

Frederick   Oh please! Don't think of it. I was just about to ask Herr Bach to play for us once again. I am desolated you weren't here fifteen minutes ago. His Italian Concerto! A masterpiece! A masterpiece!

Voltaire   Indeed! Quite marvellous!

Frederick   Please, all of you – be seated.

They find seats.

Johann   What would you like me to play, Highness?

Frederick   Well –

He reaches into his pocket and produces the manuscript containing his theme. **Johann** *proffers his hand but* **Frederick** *hugs the paper coyly to his breast.*

Frederick   I have to tell you, Bach – I find it rather difficult to sleep these days –

Johann   I'm not surprised, Majesty.

Frederick   I'm sorry?

Voltaire *coughs nervously.*

Johann   The affairs of state must weigh heavy on a monarch's head.

Frederick   Precisely. Do you sleep well, Herr Bach?

Johann *smiles – speaks lightly.*

Johann   I did, Highness. Until your troops guaranteed a lifetime's insomnia.

Frederick   My troops?

Johann   In Leipzig.

Voltaire *looks alarmed.*

Frederick   Leipzig?

Johann   Well, it's not a big town and the nightly shouting and drunken fights often make sleep problematic.

Frederick   I'm sorry. I have heard no ill reports. I shall investigate.

Johann   There's no need, Highness! It was an honour to be part of your invasion – even at its tail end.

Frederick   Invasion?

Johann   Of Silesia.

Frederick   You see my intervention as an invasion?

Johann   Intervention . . . invasion! The important thing was to suppress the country and it seems you achieved that admirably. I congratulate you.

Quantz, **Benda**, *and* **Graun** *are deeply embarrassed. The tension in the room is palpable.*

Frederick   You don't approve?

Johann   I am a humble cantor, Majesty. It's hardly my place to approve or disapprove.

Frederick   My timely excursion to Silesia, dear Bach, was simply to reclaim Prussian territory long sequestered by Austria –

Johann   Of course.

Frederick   – And I could lead you, step by step, through every decision, every legal argument, every deliberation and codicil that led to that irrevocable conclusion.

Johann *catches* **Voltaire** *staring at him. Gets the message.*

Johann   I'm quite sure it would be beyond my powers of comprehension, Majesty. I have to confess to being infinitely more intrigued by the paper in your royal hand than the complexities of war.

Voltaire   Yes, Highness. Stop tantalising us! I beg you!

Frederick *stares at* **Johann**.

Frederick   I'm not a fool, Bach. You have an issue with something. What is it?

Johann   Highness – I'm an old man. My sight is going and I have worked too hard for too long. You are a king. A great king – and you are young.

Frederick   And?

Johann   There is frankly no way that I could speak freely of my issues, my doubts –

Frederick   Why not?

Johann   The gulf between us is simply too large.

Frederick   Are you afraid?

Johann   Possibly.

Frederick   Then don't be.

Johann   Thank you. Maybe one day I shall express myself. In the meantime, let my music speak for me. Please – the paper in your –

Frederick *smiles.*

Frederick   Oh – yes! Well. The other night I was lying in bed, staring up at the ceiling, too tired to read, my head reeling with a thousand memories and concerns – when, quite suddenly, a theme came into my head – a persistent, mournful, rather beautiful theme. So I got up and wrote it down. Just like that. A few notes. Then I put it in a drawer.

A beat.

It occurred to me earlier this evening that this may be exactly the sort of theme on which you might like to improvise. May I show it to you?

Johann   Of course, Highness.

Frederick   No. I will play it.

He goes to the harpsichord and picks out the notes of his theme.

Frederick   What do you think?

Johann *is unsure how to respond.*

Johann   What kind of work did you see this becoming, Highness?

Frederick   A fugue. A three-part fugue.

Johann *frowns again. For a second he catches* **Voltaire***'s eye.*

Johann   A three-part fugue? But –

Frederick   Yes?

Johann   This is –

A beat.

Frederick   Is it possible?

Johann   I'm not completely sure, Majesty.

Frederick   You're not sure?

Johann   It's very complex.

Frederick   Complex?

Johann   Yes – chromatic, and then with this large fall to the seventh it's –

A beat.

Frederick   So –?

Johann *shakes his head in frustration.*

Frederick   Not possible?

Johann   I think not, Majesty.

An almost audible gasp of relief from the three musicians.

Frederick   Oh – how sad. You won't try?

Johann   Well, I might . . .

A moment and then **Johann** *gets up and goes to the harpsichord. He sits and bangs out the notes of the theme.*

Carl *enters quietly.* **Quantz** *sees him and stands in alarm –*

But he's pulled back down by **Benda**. **Carl** *sits in the corner of the room, unseen by* **Johann**.

Johann *looks up.* **Voltaire** *is staring straight at him.* **Johann** *catches his look.* **Voltaire** *nods imperceptibly.*

Then **Johann** *starts the theme again and this time begins to develop it a little – and then the second voice enters. He develops this and then the third voice. The playing continues – complex, effortless and endlessly inventive.*

Quantz moves to another chair. He slumps down, holding the handkerchief to his mouth. He looks at **Benda**, *who shakes his head in despair before burying his head in his hands.* **Graun** *sits motionless.*

Frederick *claps his hands for the music to stop. It does.*

Frederick   Marvellous, Bach! Brilliant! So clever! How did you do that?

Johann   With difficulty, Majesty. With great difficulty because, you see, the theme is so constructed that the harmonic options become increasingly constrained. Unless –

Frederick   Unless?

Johann   Well – I discovered that by using the bass to guide the descending chromatic steps – let me show you – like this –

Frederick   But tell me, Bach – is it not true that you have a system that interprets the meaning of a piece through its intervals?

Johann   The meaning of the piece?

Frederick   Yes. I gather you integrate biblical Gematria, Kabbalistic alphabet systems and suchlike into your compositions.

A beat.

Johann   Highness, you are a composer yourself and –

Frederick   Yes, yes but my works are very simple. I write merely to please the ear. I attribute no meaning to what I write – no theological or philosophical interpretation.

Johann   But this is your theme, is it not?

Frederick   It is.

Johann   Then, Highness – in the light of what you have just told me – why do you think there could be –?

Frederick   Some hidden meaning?

Johann   Yes.

Frederick   Well, you never know!

He laughs. **Johann** *plays the theme again.*

Johann   The theme is in C minor – a grave key that I would normally reserve for the most serious works.

A beat.

For me, Highness, music is a language; a language as meaningful as the words I am speaking now. If I speak nonsense it will remain nonsense. The same can be true of any theme in music. But your theme is not nonsense. Neither is it written to merely please the ear. It speaks of struggle, of pain and sorrow. I could elaborate on my reasons for stating this and –

Frederick   – No doubt add scriptural references to the elaboration.

A beat.

Johann   I don't see scripture or faith as divorced from life, Highness.

Frederick   Whereas I am repelled by both.

Johann *laughs.*

Frederick   Why do you laugh?

Johann   Well, my faith would be weak indeed if it was shaken by your repulsion.

Frederick   I have no desire to shake your faith, Bach. I was merely stating my position.

Johann *smiles.*

Frederick   But now – please. Improvise a six-part fugue.

Johann *stares at him.*

Johann   A six-part fugue?

Frederick   Show us your mettle.

Johann   My –?

He stops.

Frederick   Well?

Johann *closes the lid of the harpsichord and slowly gets to his feet. He is white with anger.*

Johann   Majesty, I have never written a six-part fugue – let alone improvised one. And certainly not on a theme as complex as this. A theme that could have been almost designed to defeat the player.

The company avert their eyes.

Give me pen, paper and sufficient time and I am convinced I could write it. But improvise? I'm afraid not. Perhaps one of your other eminent musicians might care to try? Herr Benda?

Benda   My dear Bach – believe me it's quite beyond my powers to improvise a three-part fugue, let alone a six-part fugue – on this theme or any other.

Johann   Herr Graun?

Graun   Like my esteemed colleague, Benda, I must decline.

Johann   Quantz?

*But **Quantz** is too miserable to reply. He simply shakes his head. **Voltaire** stands and comes to **Johann**. Takes both his hands in his.*

Voltaire   Herr Bach, I must tell you, before this illustrious company and before God, that I have never heard your like. Never. You are without a doubt the finest artist I have ever encountered.

Johann *bows his head slightly.*

Johann   I shall treasure your words. Thank you.

Voltaire *holds* **Johann***'s look. Smiles, squeezes his hands and returns to his place.* **Johann** *turns to* **Frederick***, who has moved to the window and is staring out at the gardens.*

Johann   Majesty, you invited me to speak freely. To speak without fear.

Frederick *half turns. Nods.*

Johann   There is a baker in Leipzig –

Frederick   A baker? Yes?

Carl *has taken an involuntary step forward in alarm.*

Johann   A man by the name of Kessler. He has a daughter of fourteen. She's blind. On Easter Sunday she was raped by four of your soldiers.

A silence.

Frederick   And is that why you can't sleep?

Johann   Among many things, sire. Yes.

Frederick   Well, I'm sorry. These things happen.

A beat.

Anything else?

Johann *takes a moment to recover himself.*

Johann   I believe there is still one harpsichord for me to examine. With your permission, I shall do so now.

Frederick *hardly moves.*

Frederick   Of course.

Johann *bows and makes for the door. He passes* **Carl***, who whispers fiercely.*

Carl   For God's sake . . .

Johann *turns again to face the room. He is shaking with anger.*

Johann   'These things happen'?

Frederick *has turned away. He now spins around to face* **Johann**.

Johann   Do you mean, Majesty, that they happen like the rain? Or a spring flood –

Frederick   Herr Bach –

Johann   Do you mean 'these things' are unavoidable?

Frederick   Yes!

Johann   I see.

Frederick   They are a regrettable by-product of war.

A beat.

What do you want me to do? It was Easter! They were drunk! She should have been in bed!

Johann   She had been to church. She was –

Frederick   Well, she should have been in bed! What do you want me to do?

Johann   She's blind!

Frederick   So what?

Johann   She was alone in –

Frederick   Oh for Christ's sake, Bach! She was alone, she was blind, she was cold. What else was she? Lame? Deaf? Dumb?

Johann   You asked me to speak freely and –

Frederick   And you have. You have told me about your baker and his daughter and it's all most regrettable.

Johann   Regrettable?

Frederick   Well, isn't it?

Johann   That's not a word I would have chosen.

Frederick   Alright – sad, dreadful, wicked, shameful –

Johann   Pitiless? Savage?

Frederick   Perhaps.

Johann   Vicious? Heartbreaking? Sickening? Evil? Merciless? Vile? Brutal? Contemptible? Depraved? Cruel beyond imagination? . . .

A beat.

Frederick   If you like. But what can I do?

Johann   Majesty, with respect, that's the third time you've asked that question.

Frederick   And?

Johann   Well – it's not for me to advise but – surely you could find the men who did this and punish them!

Frederick   It was two months ago, Bach! In Leipzig!

Quite suddenly **Johann** *completely loses his temper.*

Johann   I LIVE IN LEIPZIG!

Carl *takes an involuntary step towards his father.* **Voltaire** *steps forward.*

Voltaire   A wonderful city, Bach. I was there some years ago, visiting a friend in the –

Johann   I live in Leipzig! In Saxony! A city and state clearly worthy of your contempt.

Voltaire *thinks better of his interruption and steps back.*

Johann   I am the Cantor of the Thomasschule!

Carl   What are you doing –?

Johann   In Leipzig! And this happened only fifty steps from my church! In Leipzig!

Carl   Father – I think perhaps it's time we –

Johann   Not now!

Frederick *stares at him.*

Frederick   Were there witnesses?

Johann   Someone saw it from a window.

Frederick   What did they see?

Johann   It was night –

Frederick   So it was dark?

Johann   Yes.

Frederick   And she was blind? It was dark and she was blind.

He shrugs.

There is no way to identify these men.

Johann   I'm sure there would be if it had happened in Potsdam.

Johann *has gone too far and he knows it.* **Frederick** *stares at him.*

Frederick   I invited you to Potsdam, Bach, because I longed to hear you play. Also, I wanted your opinion of my keyboards. You have fulfilled both wishes admirably and I am grateful. If I had wanted your opinion as a policeman I would have asked for it.

Johann *stands for a moment. Then he bows and turns to leave.*

Frederick   You are not dismissed.

Johann *turns.*

Frederick   You think me callous and you think me cruel. Don't you?

Johann's *silence confirms it.*

Frederick   Exactly. And you are suggesting that I care nothing for the territories my army has occupied. That –

Johann   Majesty, I –

Frederick   That I allow my troops free rein – to plunder and rape at will – so long as it's far from home.

Johann   That is not what I was implying, Majesty.

Frederick   Let me be clear. I am a stern disciplinarian. I am famous for it. I was brought up with discipline and I respect it. My troops respect me because they know their limits. But war is war.

A beat.

And you have clearly never fought.

Johann   That's true, Majesty.

Frederick   Had you done so, you would understand what happens. In battle. To a man's heart . . . to his soul. The rush. The unique charge of crazed excitement that –

Johann   Permits him to rape a blind girl outside a church.

Frederick *smacks the table hard.*

Frederick   No! Why are you so consumed with this wretched girl?!

Johann   Why are you not?

With an exasperated gesture, **Frederick** *appeals to* **Voltaire***, who takes a step forward.*

Voltaire   Majesty, none of us here are soldiers. You are a great one. Probably the greatest in Europe. For you war is life. For us – we know nothing of it. Nothing. And, when we see it – it comes as a shock. A horror.

After a moment **Frederick** *turns back to* **Johann***.*

Frederick   We're talking at cross-purposes, Bach.

Johann   I don't think so.

Everyone in the room is now deeply uncomfortable.

Your men were on their way home from Silesia – where, no doubt, they behaved with equal decorum. They pointed a cannon at our city gates and asked for hospitality. Our choice was simple. Yield or die.

Frederick   This is the eighteenth century, Bach! We have to move on! We cannot sit, stagnant in the slough of history – crucified by medieval, dynastic structures. Things have to change.

Johann   Or?

Frederick   Or? Good God, man! Or we allow ourselves to be conquered! Overrun. By scum!

Johann   And that was us, was it? We were the scum. The people of Leipzig.

Frederick   That's not what I –

Johann   Even though we'd done nothing. Nothing at all.

Frederick   Bach, this wasn't an attack –

Johann   We were hundreds of miles from Silesia –

Frederick   You need to understand – none of what happened in your city was under my command. I was here. In Potsdam. A month before Easter.

The general who requested Leipzig's hospitality was Prince Leopold of Anhalt-Dessau.

Johann   Talking of medieval, dynastic structures!

Frederick *can't help smiling.*

Johann   But if, as you say, Majesty, it wasn't an attack – then what was it? Were we being punished? Or was it merely a festive stop-over? A post-battle jaunt? We've had troops in our homes, sprawled on our floors, fornicating in our attics, for weeks! Young men with limbs torn off, scarred, burned, their minds half-blown; men so drunk they'll tear each other to pieces for a glass of schnapps, who leer at our wives, drag whores in at night . . .

Frederick   Yes. The Silesian campaign took a great toll.

A beat.

We have a historic right to certain territories – lands stolen from us. A historic right! And we strike first! First! Always. First! Why?

His question is not rhetorical. He waits for an answer.

Why do we do that?

Johann   Majesty, I –

Frederick *bangs the table as he speaks.*

Frederick   Because our enemies are waiting. This is Prussia. It's different. Soon you will see. Prussia will sound the bell – the bell of improvement and progress – of strength and learning throughout Europe. You will see.

Johann   I'm afraid my sight is going, Majesty.

Frederick   Then your children will see and your grandchildren will see! A new era is dawning – and yes, there will be casualties. Regrettable things will happen. It's unavoidable. But our country is changing, day by day – I have seen it for myself. People are happier. Wealthier. We have reclaimed vast tracts of farmland, reformed agriculture, overhauled the civil service, strengthened the military – renewed faith in our national heritage. We are moving forward. Day by day.

A silence.

This man Kessler. The baker. Do you speak to him?

Johann   I buy my bread from him but –

Frederick   Where is his daughter?

Johann   I haven't seen her. Not since Easter. Nobody has.

Frederick   I will send him something. Now go. GO.

He waves a hand. **Johann** *bows and leaves.*

Carl   Majesty –

Frederick   It's alright. Believe me. I asked him to speak freely and I meant it.

He looks out into the garden.

Frederick   Is it raining?

Everyone looks out at the garden. Then **Frederick** *turns briskly.*

Gentlemen, we must pay our debts. We agreed by sunset.

He turns to **Carl**.

I shall arrange for mine to be paid directly to you, Bach.

He leaves.

Scene Six

Johann's *room. Afternoon.*

Johann *is stuffing clothes into a bag.* **Carl** *enters. He holds a sizeable leather purse, bound tightly at the neck. Puts it on the table.*

Carl   Your winnings.

Johann *looks up.*

Carl   Four thousand thaler.

A huge sum!

Johann   What are you talking about?

Carl   There was a wager and I won. Take it.

Johann   Wager?

Carl   They wagered you wouldn't be able to improvise a fugue on Fritz's theme. I wagered you would. And you did.

Johann *stares at him. Then nods.*

Johann   I don't want it.

Carl   Neither do I.

Johann   Then give it to someone who does.

He resumes his packing.

Carl   I want you to take this money.

A beat.

Take it.

Johann   Alright.

Carl *hands him the purse.* **Johann** *hurls it at the wall.*

Carl   I see.

He makes for the door.

Johann   I'm not a performing ape!

Carl *turns.*

Carl   Let me be completely clear. This was the King's conceit. Entirely. It came from him. He asked them to doctor his theme, in order to confound you. I stayed out of it. But the others tried and, self-evidently, they failed. There was a wager on the outcome and I was the only one who bet you would succeed. For that, I was locked in a room to stop me from showing you the theme. Had it not been for Emelia, I'd still be in there!

A beat.

I'm sorry I couldn't prevent any of this but, unlike yourself, I found myself unable to contradict a monarch.

Johann *returns to packing.*

Carl   Anyway, it's all fairly academic now.

Johann   Why?

Carl   Because, thanks to you, it's extremely doubtful I'll still have a position here.

Johann   You're well out of it!

Carl *picks up the purse, opens it, and tips the contents into a shallow bowl on the table. He pockets several gold coins.*

Carl   So, I may as well keep some of this. I'll need it.

Johann   Carl. Let me tell you something. This place is a Godless, shallow, irreligious –

Carl *spins on his heel, livid.*

Carl   What did you think you were doing? In there? For the love of God! You're sixty-two! How many wars have been fought since you were born? Tell me! In Saxony? In Prussia, Poland, Bohemia? How many invasions? Counter-invasions? How many revolts? How many occupations?

Johann *shakes his head.*

Carl   What do you think happened during the Pomeranian campaign?

Johann   The what?

Carl   Exactly! The siege of Stralsund! Vilnius, Krakow?

Johann *stares at him blankly.*

Carl   There are hundreds of thousands – possibly millions – of people in those places. Millions! Did you give them a passing thought? Ever? Did their suffering stop you from composing? Performing? Praying? Even for a day?

Johann *can't answer this.*

Carl   But now – quite suddenly – you can talk of nothing but Silesia! To the extent that you're prepared to challenge the King in his own palace? To jeopardise your son's livelihood? What were you hoping to gain?

A beat.

Johann   Justice.

Carl   For who? The bodies in the pits? The soldiers who died? Kessler's daughter?

There is a knock.

Enter . . .

Voltaire *enters.*

Johann   Monsieur!

Voltaire *approaches* **Johann**. *He seems to be in a hurry. Gives a little bow.*

Voltaire   Herr Bach, forgive me but I must be brief. You mentioned *Hamlet*. When I was in England I saw this play – and I own a copy. I always carry it with me when I travel.

He holds up a volume of Hamlet.

It is a towering piece of work. A masterpiece. But the lines that stay with me, far beyond the heartbreaking poetry of doubt and conscience, are these:

He opens the book at a marked page and reads:

> I see the imminent death of twenty thousand men,
> That, for a fantasy and trick of fame,
> Go to their graves like beds, fight for a plot
> Whereon the numbers cannot try the cause,
> Which is not tomb enough and continent
> To hide the slain?

'For a fantasy and trick of fame, go to their graves like beds.' Everything, Herr Bach. In one phrase.

He closes the book.

You were right and brave to confront His Majesty. Little will come of it – but you were right and brave. I salute you. Courage.

He holds out his hand and **Johann** *takes it.*

Voltaire   Life is a shipwreck but we must not forget to sing in the lifeboats. *Au revoir*, monsieur.

Johann   *Au revoir*, monsieur.

Voltaire *bows and leaves.* **Johann** *looks at* **Carl**.

Carl   Congratulations. You have the approval of the greatest philosopher in Europe.

The door opens and **Emelia** *enters.*

Emelia   Shall I come back, sir?

Johann   That's alright, Emelia. Come in.

Emelia *goes to* **Johann** *and takes a shirt from him.*

Emelia   Allow me, sir.

She goes to the chest of drawers and begins to remove clothes. She folds them and starts to place them in the bags.

Emelia   Can I enquire when you are planning on leaving, Herr Bach?

Johann   As soon as possible.

Carl   Is there a coach to Luckenwalde later today?

Emelia   I can ask. Spend the night there, Herr Bach – you could be in Leipzig by tomorrow evening.

Johann   Anything rather than stay here.

In the near distance a series of loud cannon shots.

Emelia   That'll be Babelsberg. Some manoeuvre, some war game . . .

Johann   My son says he no longer notices it. Hard to believe, even after five years.

Emelia   Count yourself lucky. My boy only had to hear a bugle and he'd want to enlist.

Johann   And did he? Enlist?

Emelia   On his fifteenth birthday. He died two years ago. Killed in action.

A beat.

Johann   Where was this?

Emelia   One of His Majesty's campaigns. Over in the East. Somewhere near Breslau.

She continues to pack his clothes.

He wanted to be a soldier. All his life. Franz. Growing up here – well you can imagine – there's nothing else. When he was small he'd follow behind when they drilled – all day. Up and down with a stick over his shoulder. Loved it. Christ knows why.

A beat.

Emelia   So he gets to fifteen and there's no stopping him.

Johann   How old was he when –?

Emelia   When he got blown to bits? Eighteen. His Majesty sent his condolences. My husband wanted us to move on – get work somewhere else, but I've been here fifty years. These people are shits. Us moving won't change that. We'd just be working for different shits.

A silence.

Carl   By the way, Emelia, once again – thank you for releasing me.

Emelia *smiles.*

Emelia   Lucky I had the spare key. But you're not the only one who's free, sir.

She points a thumb to her bosom.

Got the boot. Dismissed.

A shocked silence.

Carl   Dismissed? For unlocking a door?

Emelia   Letting you out. Insolence, disobeying a royal order –

Johann   That's an outrage!

Carl   I shall speak to the King immediately . . .

Emelia   It'll do no good, sir. His Majesty leaves that sort of thing to Herr von Meckelsdorf.

Carl   Then I shall talk to him.

Emelia   Please don't, sir. It's been coming for some time. He only needed an excuse. He gave me twenty-four hours to get out.

Carl   So where will you go?

Emelia   I don't know. This has been my home for fifty years.

Johann   Do you have any relatives?

Emelia   Only my sister.

Johann   In Leipzig. Of course! Ulrike! Married to Gustav!

Emelia   Yes, but Gustav's in jail.

Johann   Why?

Emelia   Some officer insulted Ulrike, and Gustav hit him. Broke his jaw. That's all I know. They've got five soldiers billeted in their house.

Johann   Then you can stay with us!

Emelia   Oh, Herr Bach, I couldn't –

Johann   And you can travel with me. I'll enjoy the company. Say yes.

Emelia   Herr Bach, I –

Johann   Say yes.

Emelia *beams.*

Emelia   Yes.

Suddenly **Johann** *picks up the shallow bowl and pours the remaining coins into a jug. Hands the jug to* **Emelia**.

Johann   Here.

Emelia *stares at the money in shock.*

Emelia   What's this?

Johann   Just take it.

Emelia *stares into the jug.*

Emelia   But this is a fortune! Where does it come from?

Carl   Well –

Johann   It would take too long to explain. Please –

Carl *takes the jug from* **Johann** *and presses it into* **Emelia**'s *hands.*

Carl   It's yours. Hide it in here.

Johann   It might make some sense of the last few days.

Emelia *jiggles the jug, which is clearly very heavy. She stares at father and son in wonder.*

Emelia   I don't know what to say, sir.

Johann   Just get me that coach!

Emelia *grins. She bows and leaves, holding the jug of cash.*

Blackout.

Scene Seven

A beautiful soprano voice is heard singing in Italian.

Six weeks later. Leipzig. July 1747. Thomasschule, Bach's apartment. Afternoon.

Summer heat. Fierce shafts of sunlight stream through the windows.

Anna *sits at a small keyboard singing an aria by Vivaldi.* **Johann** *reclines on a divan in his shirtsleeves. He watches her intently. The song comes to its languorous finish.*

Johann *lies staring dreamily at his wife.*

Johann   Why didn't you become an opera singer?

Anna   Mainly, I suppose, because I met you – and I've been giving birth ever since. Something along those lines.

Johann   A footling excuse.

Anna   I could have been rich. Like the Conradis in Dresden, or that Müller woman.

Johann   I'd write you such wonderful operas. London, Paris, Berlin –

Johann *grins and blows her a kiss. Then from outside comes the sharp rat-a-tat of skilful military drumming. Many snare drums.* **Johann** *scowls, jumps up and peers out of the window.*

Look at them! Lined up like sweating dolls . . . What's the point? Who cares?

Anna *gets up and lets down a linen blind on one of the windows. She pours herself a glass of lemonade from a jug on the table. Pours another for* **Johann**.

Anna   Here.

Johann *takes the glass, draws her close and kisses her. Then he drains his lemonade in one. Outside the drumming continues.* **Anna** *goes to the table and continues work, copying out a manuscript.*

Johann   Where's Emelia?

Anna   Upstairs with Regina.

Johann   Any news about Gustav?

Anna   He's been released.

Johann   God be praised! Why didn't you tell me?

Anna   Emelia wants to tell you herself. She said it couldn't have happened without you.

Johann   Me?

Anna   She used the money you gave her. Bribed one of the guards. Some man she knew from Potsdam . . .

Johann *claps his hands together. Laughs.*

Johann   The Lord moves in such mysterious ways!

Anna   She said it cost a fortune. Shouldn't you be working?

Johann   It's too hot. I handed over to Kraus. He can fight the drumming. The boys are all half-asleep anyway. I've had a letter from Carl. He's coming home for a few days.

Anna   When is he arriving?

He pours himself some more lemonade. Boys' voices are heard singing a chorale in a room below.

Johann   Tomorrow or the next day. He has permission to leave.

Anna   And does he have permission to return? To Potsdam?

Johann *sighs in irritation.*

Johann   Don't start. Carl still has his job. And – whatever I did or didn't do in Potsdam – I did it with the best of –

A cry from **Emelia** *is heard from the hall.*

Emelia   Oh dear God!

The door swings open and a breathless **Emelia** *rushes in.*

Anna   Emelia –!

Emelia   Herr Bach! Herr Bach!

She looks as though she's seen a ghost.

Johann   What? Emelia – please. Calm down. Stop. Just –

Emelia   It's . . . It's . . . he . . . he's –

And **Frederick II of Prussia** *strides into the room. He is wearing the blue uniform of a Prussian soldier. A panicked* **Emelia** *curtsies low.*

Johann *and* **Anna** *just remain sitting with their mouths open.*

Frederick   Herr Bach – Please forgive this unannounced intrusion.

Johann *stands, pulling* **Anna** *up as he does so.*

Johann   Majesty!

He bows. **Frederick** *laughs – a conjurer revealing his magic! He spins one turn on the spot.*

Frederick   I know! – Where did I come from? How did I get in? What am I doing here? Well, I followed the singing, I climbed the stairs – and there, waiting at the top, was Emelia! As though it was meant . . .

Anna *curtsies.* **Frederick** *gives her a gracious bow.*

Frau Bach – such a delight to make your acquaintance. Herr Bach – I am here incognito. Shhh! One of the advantages to being King of Prussia is that so few people have the slightest idea what I look like. I just strolled through your market square and – not a head turned. Admittedly, I kept my hat low over my eyes but . . . Heaven!

Johann *gestures to a chair.*

Johann   Please, Highness . . .

Frederick   So this is where you live! It's quite charming. Simple, elegant –

He walks to the window and stares down at the park below. From the room below the chorale increases in volume.

Frederick   Ah! What a view. Park, river, sky . . . and music. What are they singing, Bach? Something you wrote?

Johann   They're practising a chorale, Highness. But I'm afraid the infernal drumming down in the gardens, together with the heat, is making it –

Frederick   Nevertheless – it's very lovely.

Johann *nudges* **Anna**, *who pulls herself together.*

Anna   May I offer your highness some refreshment?

Frederick   That's very kind, Frau Bach. I really cannot stay long but – perhaps some of that –

Anna   Lemonade? Of course.

Frederick   Emelia! It's good to see you. Are you working here now?

Emelia   No, Highness. I was supposed to be living with my sister. But her house is full of soldiers. So Herr Bach has very kindly let me stay here until –

She catches **Johann***'s eye and stops mid-sentence.*

Emelia *curtsies on reflex. Then she pours a glass of lemonade and hands it to* **Frederick**.

Frederick   This smells delicious.

He drinks. Savours for a moment.

Frederick   Orange blossom?

Emelia   Exactly, highness!

Anna *makes eye contact with* **Johann** *and takes* **Emelia***'s arm.*

Anna   We'll leave the lemonade with you.

She skilfully manoeuvres **Emelia** *from the room. The two men are left alone.*

Frederick   It's very good to see you, Bach. You left Potsdam in such a rush.

Johann   Indeed, Majesty.

Frederick *sits. He cranes his neck a little and peers through the window at the sky.*

Frederick   I think we may have a storm before the day is out . . .

Johann   May I ask, Highness – what brings you to Leipzig?

Frederick   A number of things. There are certain matters that need my attention – some military, some governmental – and my time is very limited. But I thought – while I was in the vicinity, why not?

He gives a little laugh.

If Mohammed refuses to come to the mountain, then the mountain must come to Mohammed. If you remember, Bach, in Potsdam, I presented you with a theme on which I asked you to –

Johann   Improvise a three-part fugue. Yes. A theme that you wrote yourself. How could I forget?

Frederick   Thank you. I remember I was very taken with your assessment of my little tune. I had no idea that it was so multi-faceted . . . that it spoke to so many different . . . emotions . . . just twenty notes . . .

A silence. **Johann** *gathers his thoughts.*

Johann   As I remember, you said you were unable to sleep. And the theme just appeared. It persisted, so you wrote it down.

Frederick *nods.*

Johann   In such a circumstance, I think perhaps it was insisting you listen. To its meaning.

Frederick   Really? And tell me . . . what is that? What is 'its meaning'?

Johann   Only you can discover that, sire.

Frederick   That's rather elliptical . . . Tell me – and I'm very interested in this – do you think your faith enabled you to improvise a three-part fugue on my theme?

Johann   No more than your lack of it prompted you to confound my attempt.

Frederick *smiles.*

Frederick   Touché.

A beat.

My dear Bach . . . the wager was a joke! An innocent bit of fun . . . which, by the way, earned your son a handsome purse.

Johann   Sire, if I persuaded you to mount a horse, which I strongly suspected might throw you, and then secretly wagered on the result – I imagine you might feel somewhat used. Whatever the outcome.

Frederick   Possibly. But being thrown from a horse can cause severe injury. Whereas . . .

He gives a chuckle.

What an argumentative fellow you are! Aren't you? First my soldiers' behaviour in Leipzig, then your wounded pride . . . I wonder what will ruffle your feathers next?

Johann   With respect, sire, you are now *in* Leipzig. Your 'soldiers' behaviour', as you put it, happened here – and, I regret to say, continues to do so. The incident I described was an act of barbarism.

Frederick *looks uncomfortable.*

Frederick   I have only your account of this episode but –

Johann   You need only speak to the girl's father, her mother, her brother, the neighbours –

Frederick   As I said, I will make enquiries –

Johann   There's a brothel up the road. They could have gone there. Instead, they attacked a blind girl in the street. To be precise – in that park. They knew exactly what they were doing.

Frederick   Did they?

Johann   How could they not?

Frederick   Well . . .

He sighs. Shrugs.

I suppose we must always take the circumstances into account. If, for example, a soldier, having spent months fighting through blood and fire, steals some trifle, or decides to have a bit of fun with a woman, then that is surely understandable, though . . .

Johann   A bit of fun with a woman?

Frederick   Nobody's saying it's excusable . . . but it's human! Surely you can see that? Flawed of course but –

Johann   The soldiers who crucified Christ were human!

Frederick   Oh, please! Not now.

Johann   Was what they did 'understandable'? I suppose so. They were, after all, just doing their job. But a catastrophe nevertheless.

Frederick *has become suddenly agitated.*

Frederick   You see, Bach – this is precisely why I can't take your religion. Its central image is so disgusting. 'Forgive them, Father – they know not what they do.' That's nonsense! Isn't it? Surely it should be, 'Forgive them, Father – they know exactly what they do'? Isn't that the central point?

Johann   They were murdering the son of God!

Frederick   Yes, but they didn't believe in his divinity, did they? Neither do I. They were torturing a fellow human being to death and they knew precisely what they were doing. So why should there be any forgiveness for that?

A beat.

I have abolished torture. And I go to war to protect my kingdom, to improve the conditions of my subjects. In the process, terrible things happen – and I'm sorry for that. But terrible things would happen if I didn't go to war. Life is hard.

A beat.

I'm sorry, Bach. I cannot pretend to believe something I simply do not. I know my views offend you but –

Johann   I'm not offended. And what difference would it make if I was? It's only that –

A beat.

I suppose . . .

He stops. Shakes his head. **Frederick** *waits – then, quite suddenly, stands up.*

Frederick   Bach – listen to me. If we're to talk, then it must be man-to-man. Do you understand? I am in your home!

A moment and he sits again.

Please try to forget who I am. You're free to say whatever you feel. I mean it.

Johann *looks at him. Shrugs.*

Johann   Christ's resurrection means nothing to you?

Frederick   It's not that it means nothing to me. I just don't believe it.

A beat.

And does that then preclude all further conversation?

Johann   Not at all but . . .

Frederick   Tell me, Bach – feeling as you do – why did you come to Potsdam?

Johann   Sire, I was profoundly honoured to receive such an invitation and deeply mortified to discover that –

Frederick   Can we cut the frills? Please get to the point.

A beat.

Johann   I came to see my son . . . to visit my grandchildren in Berlin and to meet you, sire.

Frederick   In that order?

Johann   Not necessarily. I was very curious to meet you but deeply conflicted.

Frederick   You have my word. I will look into these events in Leipzig.

A beat.

By the way, how are your eyes? Have you had the operation?

Johann   Not yet. Dr Taylor is due here in a few days. I'm not exactly relishing the prospect, but –

Frederick   Ugh! Let's not dwell on it. Now – in Potsdam before you left in such a rush, we were talking about meaning. In music. About your interest in numerology, in biblical gematria, mathematics, cryptography –

Johann   True. Some disciplines can, quite spontaneously, reveal the divine clockwork ticking behind every second of our lives. And one of those is music. Certain music can knock at the heart's door, bid it open and translate God's word straight to the soul. How it does that I have no idea. But it has the power to do so. And to do so more immediately and more profoundly than anything I know. That is its meaning.

Frederick   But 'meaning'? Meaning about what? Meaning about meaning?

Johann *shrugs.*

Johann   I study scripture. Constantly. I make no apology for that. There is no other meaning.

Frederick   Then, what? Our relation to God?

Johann   Our experience of God.

Frederick   And what if we don't believe in Him?

Johann   That has no bearing on his presence – or his existence. Only on your lack of faith.

Frederick   I see. So, your belief proves His existence?

Johann   Or vice-versa. Yes.

Frederick   Oh, for God's sake!

Johann *grins. There is a roll of thunder. They both smile at its spooky timing.*

Johann   And yet – you see – you were visited.

Frederick   Visited?

Johann   By your theme. A theme you had never previously heard – and yet seemed to speak to you – albeit in another tongue – and which you suspect may have meaning. Its enigma continues to haunt you – and now, even six weeks later, your search for its significance has brought you here.

Frederick *nods slowly.*

Johann   Where do you think it came from?

Frederick   Where do dreams come from? Thoughts? Memories? It's a mystery.

Johann   Indeed. But it materialised within *you*. Nobody else. Music certainly contains meaning, but its messages are spiritual, emotional and completely non-rational.

He progresses tentatively.

Which is why, I think, your theme emerged. And why you felt compelled to write it down. And, perhaps, why you presented me with the challenge of turning it into a fugue. Maybe you hoped, in the process, it might reveal itself.

Frederick   As what?

Outside, raindrops can be heard spattering the window.

Reveal itself as what?

Johann   Perhaps – as –

As if on cue, the crash of military drumming outside, accompanied by bugles, trumpets and the scream of orders. **Frederick** *suddenly smashes his hand down hard on the table.*

Frederick   Bach! What? Reveal itself as what?

Johann *moves to the keyboard and picks out the theme. He smiles ironically.*

Johann   As . . . Something frail . . . Something small, defenceless, unlovely, unloveable – . . . emerging from deep within . . . Wounded. Alone . . . something that speaks of struggle, of pain, of grief – and looks for the hopeful resolve of those emotions.

The drumming outside increases in volume.

The total opposite of what's happening out there . . . the opposite of whatever it is that drives you constantly onto the battlefield.

The marching bands outside increase in volume. **Frederick** *sits as if frozen. Then the marching and music suddenly stop.*

Frederick *stands.* **Johann** *gets up.* **Frederick** *walks to the window. Stares out at the rain.*

Frederick   Torrential . . .

Then he turns. Smiles.

Frederick   *Tempus fugit.* I must go.

And before **Johann** *can bow the king is moving across the room. He turns at the door.*

Frederick   So good to see you again, Herr Bach. Good luck with your operation.

And he's gone.

Scene Eight

Five days later. Leipzig. July 1747. A parlour. Late afternoon.

The blinds are down. Hot afternoon sunshine peeps through the slats. **Johann** *sits alone. He wears a bandage around his eyes.* **Carl** *enters, holding a sheaf of manuscripts.*

Johann *reacts to the sound of the door opening.*

Johann   Who is it?

Carl   Me.

Johann *listens to his approaching footsteps.*

Johann   When does your carriage leave?

Carl   In about an hour. It's good to see you sitting up. How's the pain?

Johann *drops his head and shakes it despairingly from side to side. Then he suddenly grabs at the bandage.*

Carl   What are you doing?

Johann   What does it look like?

Carl   Taylor said you should keep it on for a week. He said –

Johann   It's unbearable! I'm not wearing it –

Carl *grips* **Johann**'s *wrist.*

Carl   Stop! Please.

He is too strong. **Johann** *stops. His head slumps forward.*

Carl   When is Taylor coming back?

Johann   Hopefully never.

Carl   Well, you either listen to him or you –

Johann   Carl, I'll tell you why he wants me to wear this filthy rag for a week. Because by then he'll be a hundred miles away and he won't have to account for the damage he's done.

Carl   What damage?

Johann   The man's wasted in medicine. He should work in an abattoir.

Carl   What damage?

Johann   I'm blind!

Carl   Oh – that's nonsense –

Johann   Carl! For the love of God!

Anna *enters carrying a small tray. On the tray is a bowl of water, a small pot of ointment and several lint cloths.*

Anna   Why is your bandage half-off?

Johann   It's making me feel sick!

Anna   Dr Taylor said –

Johann   I know what Taylor said!

Johann   Then listen to him!

Johann   There are blind men all over Europe who listened to Taylor.

Anna   He said the light could damage your eyes –

Johann   What light?

Anna   Johann – please –

She places the tray on a small table. **Carl** *quickly changes the subject.*

Carl   Anna, my father has asked me to take these manuscripts back to Potsdam. I need to speak with him before I –

Anna   Of course.

She removes the bandage from **Johann**'s *eyes. She takes some lint and soaks it in the water.* **Johann** *winces.*

Anna   Head back –

Johann *tips his head back.* **Anna** *begins to gently bathe his eyes.* **Carl** *watches for a moment.*

Carl   Father, listen – I've been here for three days. Why didn't you show me this before?

Johann   I was busy having my eyes out.

Anna   Stop being melodramatic. Keep your head still.

Carl   But when did you compose all this?!

Johann   In the last few weeks.

Carl   A 'Musical Offering'? It sounds like something you'd burn on an altar.

Johann   Ah, but on what altar? And to what God?

Carl *leafs through the large pile of manuscripts. Shakes his head in disbelief.*

Carl   It's incredible! I counted a six-part fugue, ten canons, a flute sonata, two more fugues – a trio sonata . . . and all based on the King's theme. All of them. I don't understand. How did this happen? You left Potsdam in such a whirlwind of fury and disgust.

Johann   True. Life is strange.

Anna *continues to bathe* **Johann**'s *eyes.*

Carl   And – then there are all these canons!

Johann   Ten of them.

Carl   One for each commandment?

Johann   No comment. Look at the top of number nine.

Carl *leafs through to number nine.*

Carl (*reads*)   'Quaerendo invenietis' – 'Seek and you shall find'.

Johann   Exactly.

Carl *picks up the title page of the whole collection.*

Carl   'A Musical Offering'. 'Regis Jussu Cantio et Reliqua Canonica Arte Resoluta'.

Anna *ties the bandage firmly around* **Johann**'s *eyes.*

Anna   'At the King's Command, the Song and the Remainder Resolved with Canonic Art'.

Johann   But . . . look at the Latin. The first letter of each word –

Carl   Regis Jussu Cantio et Reliqua Canonica Arte Resoluta. R-I-C-E-R-C-A-R.

Johann   Ricercar. It's an acrostic! (*NB: pronounced 'Richicar'.*)

Carl   But 'Ricercar'? What does it mean?

Johann   It's an ancient instruction – a practice somewhat rediscovered in the Renaissance. It means 'to seek'. To seek within.

Carl (*reads on*)   'May Your Majesty deign to dignify the present modest labour with a gracious acceptance, and continue to grant Your Majesty's Most August, Royal Grace, to Your Majesty's most humble and obedient servant. Johann Sebastian Bach. Leipzig, July 7th, 1747.'

A beat.

Are you sure you want to say all this?

Johann   Are you sure you want to keep your job?

A silence. **Johann** *doesn't move.* **Anna** *speaks quietly.*

Anna   I think you should get a move on, Carl.

She exits carrying the tray.

Johann   Put it in that leather case.

Carl *sees a leather document case, gathers the manuscripts and carefully places it inside.*

Johann   Have a good journey.

Carl *kisses the top of* **Johann**'s *head.* **Johann** *squeezes his hand.* **Carl** *takes the document case and makes for the door. But halfway across the room, he hesitates. Then, almost as an afterthought, he takes a step forward and speaks to us:*

Carl   In Potsdam, this 'Musical Offering' was placed on a shelf. It lay there for many years.

The Ricercar again begins to swell – mysterious and gracious – and then, in the distance, the sound of marching feet.

Carl   The King never opened it. He was busy. This time in Poland.

He exits. **Johann** *hears the door close. Sits, motionless. The music increases in volume, but so does the marching – until eventually the music is drowned out altogether. The sound of thousands of men marching.*

The lights fade slowly to black.

The end.